ALIVE AND KICKING

ALIVE

and

KICKING

Clare Woodward

TREGOLWYN

Copyright © Clare Woodward 2000
First published in 2000 by Tregolwyn
PO Box 11, Cowbridge
Glamorgan, CF71 7XT

Distributed by Gazelle Book Services Limited
Falcon House, Queen Square
Lancaster, England LA1 1RN

The right of Clare Woodward to be identified as the author of the work has been asserted herein in accordance with the Copyright, Designs and Patents Act 1988.

All rights reserved. This book is sold subject to the condition that it shall not, by way of trade or otherwise, be lent, resold, hired out or otherwise circulated without the publisher's prior consent in any form of binding or cover other than that in which it is published and without a similar condition including this condition being imposed on the subsequent purchaser.

All of the characters in this book are fictitious and any resemblance to actual people, living or dead, is purely coincidental.

British Library Cataloguing in Publication Data
A catalogue record for this book is available from the British Library

ISBN 0-9538688-1-8

Typeset by Amolibros, Watchet, Somerset
This book production has been managed by Amolibros
Printed and bound by T J International Ltd, Padstow, Cornwall

CHAPTER ONE

Staff Nurse Watts glared across at the woman in the bed as she stooped to clear away the tray with its half-eaten meal. Such a waste of food. Her mother would have cried to see it. These attempted suicides were often difficult. It wasn't easy to feel any sympathy for them—and it was unnecessary really, when they were so busy feeling sorry for themselves.

"Not hungry again?" she asked, rhetorically, making a cursory attempt at warmth.

"No," replied the patient, glancing up briefly from the magazine she was reading, or rather the magazine whose pages she was mechanically turning without absorbing their contents.

"I need to take your blood pressure," said the nurse, putting the tray to one side and taking out the apparatus.

"Again?" The woman threw down the magazine impatiently and raised red, tired eyes to look at her with an expression that somehow combined anger and indifference.

"I'm afraid so."

The process of fastening the band around the arm and inflating it took time and killed the need for forced conversation, but when it was over Nurse Watts allowed herself another attempt.

"Doctor will be around to see you in about an hour," she said. "He'll be bringing someone with him to talk to you."

The woman was looking at her magazine again, her lips set in a determined grimace. "That'll be nice," she said, after a momentary pause that suggested she had made a concerted effort to think of some sarcastic response.

The nurse bit her lip. "We're only trying to help you, you know."

The woman nodded slowly, without looking up.

"Help me to do what, exactly?"

Nurse Watts found she couldn't answer as easily as she had expected. "To…well, to get on with your life. To find a reason for living."

"You needn't bother. There isn't one. Not for me, anyway."

The nurse made no attempt to respond to this. Instead, she opened the small wardrobe and hung up the cardigan that had been flung down on the chair. She knew the patient didn't want it hung up, but she didn't feel disposed to make herself agreeable to this one. Besides, she loved the feel of the garment. It was what the shops label a "luxury fabric". The few other things in the wardrobe were of similar quality. This woman was not short of money. It was hard to understand how someone with such advantages in life could have lost all interest in it.

"Your mother's brought some lovely things in for you to wear when you're feeling better," she said, grasping at straws.

"You can have anything you fancy," came the reply. "I don't want them."

"The patient isn't very communicative," warned Dr Best as he led Mrs Penhaligon towards the small private room. "It's difficult to get a handle on anything, if you know what I mean. I've got children myself. I can understand so well how she must feel."

"I'm not here to dissuade her from trying again," Mrs Penhaligon replied, rather unexpectedly. "I can only listen to her, give her an outlet for her feelings. If she really wants to do it, then she will do it sooner or later. You're not responsible."

He had heard this kind of thing from psychiatrists before. Mrs Penhaligon was a little different from the usual, though. Attractive, he thought, yet brittle. The last person one would expect to be counselling suicidal patients. Actually, he found it a refreshing change from the usual oozing of sympathy.

"Mrs Grant," he said, opening the door cautiously. "Here we are. Did Nurse tell you that I'd be bringing someone to see you?"

Julia Grant, as usual, appeared unimpressed.

"A psychiatrist, I suppose," she commented, regarding his companion with indifference.

"How do you do, Mrs Grant," said the counsellor, stepping forward to take the initiative. "I'm Nora Penhaligon. And I'm not a psychiatrist."

Surprisingly (to the doctor's mind at least), Julia extended her hand in response, though her handshake was limp and unenthusiastic. It seemed to be the right kind of start.

"Your blood pressure is still not quite right," he commented, glancing briefly over the chart at the end of the bed. He looked at her. "How are you feeling—physically, I mean?"

She opened her mouth as if to answer, then changed her mind and turned her head.

"I'll leave you with Mrs Penhaligon, then," he said, after a moment. The visitor nodded, and gave him a slight smile as he backed out of the room.

She sat down beside the bed.

"Do you know why I'm here?" she asked, in a brisk voice that rejected the possibility of not receiving an answer.

"You want to make sure I don't try it again."

"Are you intending to?"

Julia gave a bitter smile. "Yes, of course. Why wouldn't I?"

Evading the question, Nora opened a buff folder and looked over several word-processed sheets.

"Do you mind if I call you Julia?" she asked, without looking up. "I prefer to be informal. And I'd like you to call me Nora."

"Does this mean you might be coming again? Only I was hoping to get away with just the one visit. Otherwise it's just a waste of your time. If you tell me what I'm supposed to say, I'll say it and you can go away with a clear conscience."

"Conscience doesn't come into this job," replied Nora, aware that Julia was watching her curiously as she leafed through the papers in the folder. Notes on this kind of case were seldom adequate, she found. "Lost husband and two children in car accident" told one nothing about the person who was suffering, nothing about her personality. Nor did "Refuses to eat, will not answer questions" throw any more light on the subject.

"Cards on the table, Julia," she said suddenly. "If you're determined to kill yourself, then I can't stop you, you'll find a way. I'm not here for that. All I can do is listen. And it may be that by talking things over with me, you'll find a way through this time and start to believe that there's some point in life. Believe it or not, it has been known to happen. I'd prefer it that way; I make no secret of it. But if I can't help you, if you truly can't see any point in going on, it won't be on my conscience. I've done too much of this to allow every failure to cause me personal anxiety and remorse. If I start to feel responsible for you, then I won't be able to help other people. So let's forget that side of it. Okay?"

She paused. Julia's eyes filled up with tears. It was hard to believe that her body was still capable of manufacturing them, so many had been cried already. Yet here they came again.

"I'm sorry. I know it's not your fault. I don't mean to be difficult, only I can't—see—any—point." The last few words were punctuated with quiet sobs.

Nora would have liked to be able to cry with her. This woman was still holding so much back.

"Don't worry about it," she said casually. "I'd prefer you to be frank with me. Say anything you like. I won't take offence. I know it's nothing personal."

"Hah." The sound that emerged was close to a laugh, if laughter had been possible for a person who had lost everything she valued in life.

"What I'd like to do, Julia," Nora went on quickly, ignoring the tears, since there was a supply of tissues close at hand, "is to get you to talk through everything and tell me what you're feeling. It's not going to be easy, but the idea isn't to re-live the past, or at least not the bad bits only. It's just to help you get some of it out of your system, so that you can perhaps get some rest, get back on your feet, and give time a chance to heal *some* of what you're suffering."

She was extra careful with her words. One didn't often meet a person who had so little to live for, and it would be a mistake to try to console in this case.

"I appreciate that," Julia said hoarsely, tears still streaming down her cheeks, but the mental barrier temporarily broken. "I'll try. But I don't think it'll work."

Later, in the hour of quiet between Nora Penhaligon's departure and the evening visiting session, Julia reflected on the possibility of some kind of friendship with this woman. Nora was quite a different kind of woman from herself—confident, almost brassy, not at all like some of the people she had spoken to before: Samaritan volunteers, counsellors, acquaintances who tried to offer sympathy and support and ended up avoiding her because in the end they lost patience with her moods and her rudeness.

The session had, she admitted to herself, had some kind of cathartic effect, though the pouring out of feelings had been too painful not to be checked at some point. She couldn't go on talking about it ad infinitum, there was just too much to be said. Nora hadn't asked her about the specifics of last winter's events, but had gone into apparent irrelevancies such as the state of her marriage at the time, her relationship with her sons, things that she hadn't wanted to think too deeply about.

This evening Julia's mother and father would visit, as usual. If her heart had not already been broken, she would have been devastated by the thought of the pain she was causing them. It was, of course, akin to what she would have felt for her own children. That didn't make it any easier to be responsive to their efforts to "help". Her mother would say the usual things: "I met Mrs so-and-so today. She was asking after you. She really thinks a lot of you," or "When you're feeling better, we'll all have a nice holiday in Norfolk with Rebecca." These pathetic attempts to lift her mood, not to accept the reality that she had nothing to live for, gave her nothing but sorrow. She didn't want to cause her parents any more pain than they had already endured.

In spite of all that, they still had a reason to live. They had another child, another daughter. No parent gives up life lightly while there are still children. Rebecca might not be able to supply them with grandchildren, but that only increased the need for their continued presence and support. If anything, Rebecca was the one whose life was empty. And even Rebecca still had Gordon.

The shock they gave her that evening was something Julia could not have foreseen in a hundred years. They had known that it would be, yet thought, in their misguided way, that it might help alleviate her depression. This was her mother's idea, she guessed. Her father, left to himself, would probably not have mentioned it.

"We've had some wonderful news," said her mother, after a few minutes of idle introductory comments. "About Rebecca. Can you guess what it is?"

"At least," her father broke in, "*we* think it's good news, and we hope you'll think the same."

"I can't imagine," she replied, pretending to care.

"She's having a baby."

Julia stared. "Are you sure?"

Her mother's eyes brightened even more at the apparent interest. "She told me herself on the phone this morning. It's quite definite. She waited until she was sure before telling us. In fact, she didn't want me to tell you. She thought it might upset you. But I know you'll be happy for her—you are, aren't you?"

"Happy? Of course." Julia knew that her face told a different story, but her mother would see what she wanted to see. Her father was looking on anxiously. She forced herself to continue the conversation. "When is it due?"

"In March. She's only two months pregnant."

"But how can she be? I thought the treatment failed. Mum, are you quite sure?"

It wasn't that she didn't want it to be true. It wasn't that she resented her sister's happiness. It wasn't.

"Yes, it seems they—the clinic—hadn't done everything they could have. They had another idea. It was a last resort, and it worked!"

"What, exactly?"

"Oh, I don't know, don't ask me what it was, she didn't go into much detail and you know I don't understand scientific things. It doesn't matter, does it, as long as she's finally able to have a baby? She didn't want to tell us yet, until she was quite sure everything was all right. She was afraid something might go wrong. But it won't, I know it won't. I've prayed…" Her volubility seemed to lose its momentum all of a sudden, and she subsided into an expectant silence.

Julia had seen her father wince at intervals throughout the conversation. To him, everything was not "all right", and wouldn't be right until Julia was better. He knew, as well as she did, that she would never recover. Her mother, on the other hand, was optimistic to an unreasonable degree. Though she had never belittled what her older daughter was going through, she firmly believed that she could get her to "snap out of it" by finding her some other interest in life—preferably in the form of a replacement husband. After all, as Mum would have said if she had dared, she and Dad were getting over the loss of their grandchildren, slowly but surely, and if they could do it, Julia could too. She was still young.

Mum and Dad had done their grieving. Somehow, Julia had expected that they would feel it more deeply than they seemed to have—not that she wanted them to suffer as she was doing, but all the same it was not as she would have expected. They had adored the boys, had been willing to devote an extraordinary amount of time to them. Yet they seemed, in the end, to be able to cope with the loss. It was something to be grateful for.

It wasn't as though Mum and Dad had liked Keith all that much. They were considerate towards him as a son-in-law, but he had never become a substitute son in the way Gordon, their other son-in-law, had. It was especially noticeable after the boys were born. In them, their grandparents had the best of both worlds: Jeremy, coming up to fifteen, tall, good-looking, quiet and studious; Andrew, just turned ten, mischievous, clever, funny and charming. Between the two of them, they epitomised all that was good about the male gender. And they were gone, and all that goodness and beauty with them.

Whenever Julia found herself beginning to think of their deaths, of what they must or might have known about it, she had to make a major effort to change the course of her thoughts, otherwise the pain was just too much to bear and she would clutch at her chest and moan. She did so now, invisibly and inaudibly, before turning her mind back to the matter in hand.

"Becky must be so thrilled," she said.

"Yes, isn't it fantastic? You're going to have a little niece or nephew in March. Now *there's* something to look forward to."

Julia looked at her father, who turned his head away, embarrassed.

So they would no longer be without grandchildren. Rebecca and Gordon would no longer be without children. Julia would have a child relation to take an interest in. Was that a reason to live? For the moment, perhaps, she would let it pass for one.

CHAPTER TWO

It was the following evening that her parents telephoned to say they couldn't visit. Auntie Pat was staying with them, and she had wanted to come along, but was too tired after her journey. They didn't like to leave her alone in the house. Julia's mother didn't drive, and her father wouldn't have dreamed of coming on his own. He had never learned how to talk to her properly. They would come tomorrow, with Auntie Pat in tow.

Despite the plausibility of the excuse offered, Julia knew the truth. Auntie Pat didn't want to come and see her. Which was just as well, because she didn't want to see Auntie Pat either. Garrulous, tactless Auntie Pat was afraid—and justifiably so—of saying something to upset Julia, especially after hearing the news of Rebecca's baby. Her brother, Julia's dad, was only too pleased to go along with it and keep her away. It was a damage limitation exercise.

Apologetic as her parents were for missing visiting hour for this, the first time, Julia was slightly relieved. They didn't *need* to come every night. It had been an effort not to break down when they started talking about Rebecca's baby. Every moment of her own pregnancies had been re-lived inside her mind, from the moment she rang her mother and said, "Start knitting," (she had not known how else to put it) to the moment her second and last child emerged into the air, legs drawn up and tiny fists clenched, and Keith remarked, "He looks like a space invader." Over the years, she had felt only very slight regret at the knowledge that she would never have another. She had encouraged Keith to have the operation a few years later. After all, they didn't want any accidents in their mid-thirties.

Now she was forty-one, too old to think about it even if she had been married, which she wasn't, not now. She, Julia Grant, aged forty-one, was a widow. A "young widow" was the phrase people sometimes used to describe women like herself. They were few and far between. Divorce was much more common, and divorcees were more in demand socially. With them, the conversation could drift into troubled waters, but it was nothing compared to the risk of upsetting a woman who had lost her entire family to the grim reaper.

It was strange, as she often thought after the event, that Owen Richards should have chosen this precise evening to visit her. She hadn't seen him since long before the accident, and hadn't expected ever to see him again. For a moment, she barely recognised him; and even when she did, she assumed he had come to visit someone else and had by chance entered the wrong room.

Owen had taught Julia to use a computer, two or three years ago now. She had taken it up mainly so that she could understand what the boys were studying at school, but these days it was second nature, so much so that she couldn't think how she had ever been baffled by the technology. Now that it was no longer any use to her, information technology was easy. She used it every day—when she could be bothered to get out of bed, that is.

Strange, too, to think that at first she had not even liked Owen. His sharp Welsh tongue, his sarcasm, so much the mirror of her own, had thrown her completely. After the first couple of classes, she remembered saying to another student, "He needs to lighten up a bit." That other person's name was long forgotten—he hadn't lasted more than another week or two, but Julia had stayed the whole course. Academic study never did hold any terrors for her. Every examination she had ever tried, she had sailed through easily.

She actually enjoyed the challenge of getting her Cobol program to work, even if all it did was calculate the repayment terms for some imaginary mortgage, the kind of thing she would never again have to worry about in real life.

Technically, Owen was not responsible for the course. That was overseen by a lecturer, who, though pleasant and sincere, did not have the gift of making people want to learn. His jokes were feeble, his explanations clumsy. Owen was a senior technician in the computer lab, just there to make sure everything was in working order. The lecturer had him on hand during practical sessions to assist in answering the students' queries, since he himself could not easily get round them all. Even when the numbers thinned out after the first four or five weeks, Owen still hovered around, ready with practical advice, and it was to him that Julia and her classmates naturally addressed their questions. For he was always there when he was wanted, and he never minded being asked.

Not that Owen was a man who suffered fools gladly. Julia had seen him lose patience with the lecturer once or twice. When she had got used to his manner, however, she realised that he was unfailingly considerate, particularly towards the female section of the class, some of whom were the kind of women that Julia always felt gave their sex a bad name. Dizzy was the most flattering term some of them merited, and she felt a compulsion to be scathing about them. Soon she discovered that, despite the banter Owen was prepared to enter into with her (knowing her capable), he would quickly take her down a peg or two if she made snide remarks about any of her fellow students.

Yes, it was true; she had been attracted to him. He might have been a few years younger than her. (How old would he be now? About thirty-four or thirty-five, she calculated.) He might not have been very much to look at, with his spiky red hair and pale complexion. But there was much to recommend him, and Julia had been very aware of it throughout their brief association.

She forgot him quickly, as one does, but he came to mind sometimes, and fondly. Once or twice she had seen him in town, and stopped to say hello. Then he had moved house, and they no longer went to the same shops. That was the end of their friendship, if you could call it that, and she had never thought for a moment of seeing him in this place. This evening, as Owen walked towards her bed, she wondered who it was he had come to the hospital to see, and how he had known she was here, in this small private room.

"Hello," he said, a little nervously, not quite looking her in the eye. "I hope you didn't mind me coming."

She could not smile, but she found her voice just enough to say, "This is very unexpected. What are you doing here?" She didn't mean to sound unwelcoming, but the effect was inevitable.

He showed no sign of taking offence. "I saw one of your friends from the programming course the other day. They told me about you—about what had been happening to you. I kept thinking about you, so I phoned up the hospital to ask after you. They mentioned that your usual visitors weren't coming tonight and you'd probably be on your own. So I thought I might—you know—come and see how you were. I hope you don't mind." He was repeating himself, a sign of the tension that showed itself only in subtle ways.

"I was going to bring some flowers," he added, "but then I thought—well, I didn't know if it would be right."

Owen might not have lost his gauche charm, but now he came into the same category as every other man she had ever looked at in the whole duration of her marriage to Keith. She felt ashamed to think that she had not valued what was genuinely hers, but instead had looked around and coveted—yes, coveted was the word the Bible used—the property of other women.

"How's Jenny?" she asked, forcing herself back into the present. Julia had only met Owen's dark, petite girlfriend on one occasion, a communal outing to the pub after an evening's lectures.

"Fine. She's still doing her BEd. I'm lecturing now, did you know? We've moved nearer the college."

She searched around for other topics of conversation. Connubial bliss was not a subject she could tolerate for long these days.

CHAPTER THREE

So, you see, I can't kill myself. Not just yet, anyway. I couldn't put Becky through that, when she's waited so long to have a child."

"You nearly did, the other day," replied Nora coolly.

"I know. It was different when I didn't know she was pregnant. I was only thinking of myself."

"So you're going to have a new niece or nephew. Your feelings about that must be rather ambivalent."

Julia was glad there was no pressure on her to feel good about Rebecca's child. It would have been a mistake on Nora's part to try that line.

"Yes, of course I've got mixed emotions, it makes me think about my own children." Her voice began to tremble, but she kept herself under control. "My mother and father think that Becky's baby can be a substitute for what I've lost. It will be for them, I suppose."

"I'm sure they feel it too, Julia. You're not being entirely fair to them."

"I know."

They were both silent for a few minutes while Nora Penhaligon looked for a new angle on what she had just been told.

"You're not going to kill yourself, then."

"No. Not now. At least, not until Becky's had the baby. And I suppose not for a while after that."

"So how will you cope?"

It was a sensible question, Julia felt, and one to which she needed to give serious thought.

"I'll have to try and see it as a reason to go on."

"Mmm." Nora was turning ideas over in her mind, unconcerned about the long pauses in the conversation.

"Does that mean I can come out of hospital?"

"As long as I'm satisfied that you're sincere."

Julia was irritated. "What the hell does it matter to you anyway? If I want to kill myself, why should you care?"

"I don't. I'm just trying to do my job properly."

There was no answer to that. Julia was infuriated by Nora's calmness. Perhaps it was deliberate, a tactic for getting her annoyed so that she got things out of her system. Or perhaps it was just Nora's natural response. Either way, she was not likely ever to get close enough to the woman to find out.

"If the doctor says you can come out," continued Nora, "then I've got no objection. Obviously, if you change your mind and end up in here again…"

"There's no danger of that. I can't wait to get out of this bloody dressing-gown. If I change my mind, as you put it, I'll do the job properly next time. I really did mean to kill myself, you know. It wasn't a cry for help."

"I appreciate that. You couldn't know that someone was going to find you in those circumstances."

Julia thought back. The day she had taken the overdose, she had genuinely not expected to be found out. Everything was prepared, down to the smallest detail. The note to her parents, telling them where she had left all her documents, and apologising in advance for any upset she might cause them. The room, warm and comforting and dimly lit, with Delius on the CD player, ready to welcome her into the next world (if there was one) or at least into eternal rest. The exact dose necessary, calculated by intensive research on the subject of suicide methods. Even the way she felt then, even with her strong desire to die, the thought of hanging herself or throwing herself under a train was repulsive. Messy. Someone else would have to clean her up off the rails. Someone else would have to walk in and find her strung up, with a blue face and her tongue hanging out. Jumping off a cliff was a possibility, but that was an impulse action, and the time for it had gone by. So it was pills or nothing.

Genuinely though, or sincerely as Nora might have put it, she had not intended to be saved. The next-door neighbour was a busybody, she knew that, but she could not have foreseen that the old woman would become suspicious about getting no answer when she knocked, even though the light was on. Lots of people left the light on when they went out at night, as a security measure, and the radio too. Julia had reckoned without Edie Mayberry's detailed knowledge of her movements, however. She had no awareness of being watched from behind the net curtains when she went out or returned, no sense that anyone else was interested in her life. Apart from her parents, that is, and she had thoughtfully picked a time when they were conveniently away seeing her sister, unlikely to phone or to pay an impromptu visit. She had left a suitable message on the answerphone. And they could not possibly get back until after she was dead.

So she owed her continued existence on earth to Mrs Edie Mayberry. She couldn't find it in her heart to hate the woman, though she had never exactly liked her. Neither could she blame the policemen who had broken in the front door, having been warned of her suicidal frame of mind by the neighbour who was more observant than she had ever imagined. She could just hear Edie telling them, "She's in there. I know she's in there." They wouldn't have believed her, of course they didn't. But they had no choice when there might be a life at stake. The car in the garage, late at night, had helped convince them. Strange to think that she had rejected the idea of dying in the car itself because she feared the noise of the engine running might alert someone to what she was doing.

And now here she was, forced to live on, weary of the endless days, mornings, evenings, all the same, aimless, meaningless, useless, without her boys. It was the boys, the loss of the boys that mattered most. Without Keith, she could have lived. Terrible to say it, but he would have understood. Any true parent loves the children more than the spouse. No competition really, however good your relationship. And Julia's relationship with Keith had been far from perfect.

Many of her friends understood, or said they did. Those with children tried hard to comfort her, whilst making strenuous efforts not to bring their own children into the conversation. Even the most sympathetic of them, however, was uncomfortable when Julia started talking about suicide. She was not so foolish as to ask any of them to help her, but she did mention it once or twice at the beginning, until she realised that it made people squirm. The prospect of becoming an accessory did not appeal to anyone, however well they understood her feelings.

She hadn't mentioned it as a cry for help. She hadn't wanted anyone to dissuade her. On the contrary, she would have appreciated a bit of encouragement. All she got, from any of them, was the usual platitudes. The best any of them could manage was to put an original turn on their way of saying it: instead of saying, "Time is a great healer" or "You've still got everything to live for" the most thoughtful of her friends said, "You want to die now, but it's possible you might change your mind." If anything, distant acquaintances were more helpful to her in these circumstances. That was why she had cut herself off from Becky, her only sister, the one most likely to understand and be moved by her plight. Time after time, Becky phoned and got monosyllabic responses to her kind enquiries. Becky must not hear anything that could give her a guilty conscience later.

Her closest friends, having known the boys and Keith in person, often couldn't think of anything to say at all. Rather than sit through the long embarrassing silences, they simply avoided seeing her. Julia wasn't hurt by this. She felt almost as sorry for them as they did for her, and knew that they stayed away, not because they didn't care, but because they cared too much. They thought of their own families, and couldn't bear to imagine the prospect of losing them and ending up like this pathetic woman.

The only ones who called regularly were Keith's partner, PJ, and his wife, Linda. Keith and PJ had been friends at university, and had gone into business together when PJ was made redundant and Keith's job looked slightly dodgy. It had been a big effort to get the capital together, but they were young then, they had energy, they didn't look at the potential difficulties, only at the advantages of being their own boss. That optimism repaid itself, and they were successful from the beginning. Julia had always liked PJ, even though she thought the shortening of his name, Patrick John, a bit of an affectation. But he had been brought up that way, a public schoolboy, confident, affable, and beneath the surface veneer, a deeply genuine man who felt for her as much as he did for himself. PJ was hurting, she could see. He had always relied on Keith for the bit of down-to-earthness that he lacked.

Linda, PJ's wife, was a different matter. Keith and PJ had actively wanted their wives to be friends, and had gone out of their way to arrange foursomes. Once they had even gone on holiday together, with the boys and PJ's two children, a boy and a girl. Martin and Victoria weren't a big hit with the Grant boys, though now, at fifteen, Vicky had developed certain obvious charms that were beginning to be noticed by both Jeremy and Andrew. Julia had found herself drawn unwillingly into a war with Linda over whose children were more talented, whose achieved more in school. Jeremy's rivals couldn't compete with his academic success, but Linda made up for it by ensuring that her kids had elocution lessons, piano lessons, violin lessons, gymnastics lessons and any other after-school activities that she could think of, the more expensive and unusual the better. They also had an au pair, a Dutch girl at the moment, whose main duties were to make sure the children didn't miss any of these activities and generally to clear up after them. Unlike Julia, Linda didn't go out to work, but she wouldn't have dreamed of letting Martin and Victoria make their own tea.

(Keith had always been telling Julia to get a cleaning lady in, but she had always declined, on the grounds that she would feel obliged to get the house into a reasonably tidy condition before any visit from a char. There would be plenty of time for housework from now on.)

Julia's irritation at Linda's pernickety domestic habits ensured that the holiday wasn't a big success, and they didn't try it again, but she was forced to go on seeing Linda socially, and found it an effort. She didn't exactly dislike Linda, but they had very little in common. Linda, to give her credit, was trying harder since Keith's death. She had even called on her own, once or twice, before the suicide attempt. However, she was the last person Julia would have gone to for advice.

Once, Julia had rung the Samaritans, though the pointlessness of that action still seized her with retrospective embarrassment. A girl who sounded about eighteen spent half an hour trying to convince her she was not suicidal. How wonderful it would be to be like that again, young, with everything in front of one, and no notion of the possible heartbreaks ahead. She ended up telling the girl (Jenny, her name was, coincidentally, though fortunately not the Jenny who lived with Owen Richards) what a great help she had been. After all, there was no need for her to suffer along with Julia, by having the phone slammed down on her and brooding for the rest of the evening on what she should have said to comfort her sad caller.

And now, here was this new baby coming into her life. A baby that belonged to someone else. No, truly, Julia didn't begrudge Becky her long-awaited happiness. She and Gordon deserved a child if anyone did. It wouldn't be around Julia much, when it was born. They lived far enough away that she would only see it on special occasions, birthdays, Christmas, that kind of thing. She would give it generous presents, make a fuss of it, become known as the favourite auntie. She would cause it to love her, like Bette Davis in that film, *The Old Maid*—though come to think of it, Bette Davis had been the real mother and it was Miriam Hopkins who had supplanted her in the child's affection.

Julia had never had any nieces or nephews before. Keith had been an only child, so there weren't many relatives on that side. His parents, she thought, were so much worse off than she was herself. He and the boys were literally all they had. It was a source of astonishment to her that they had borne it so well. But then, they had each other. They were deeply religious, members of the Presbyterian church, around which their social life (such as it was) revolved. They had, naturally, been quite shocked at Julia's attempt to take her own life. She knew this only because her mother had told her; she dreaded the day when she would have to talk to them again on the telephone. "Keith wouldn't want you to grieve for him, you know," they would say, as they had done countless times already. "You're still young, you can marry again. Keith wouldn't mind." Well, all that was true, actually, but it didn't help. Strange that people should have such totally different ways of handling bereavement.

Perhaps it was precisely because she was still "young"—or at any rate, not old—that it was so hard. She could see herself starting again with someone else. No more children, of course, that was out of the question, but possibly companionship, a sex life, a degree of fulfilment. Another forty years of life, probably. Forty empty and meaningless years, they seemed as she contemplated how she would live through them. It simply wasn't worth the bother. Apart from anything else, life was so boring now.

Becky had put her in an impossible position. There was never going to be a right time to die. Before the child was born, after it was born, on its first birthday, on its eighteenth birthday. Julia was doomed to live on, indefinitely.

CHAPTER FOUR

Julia didn't even consider driving herself home from the hospital. She hadn't wanted so much as to sit in a car since the accident, and only did so when absolutely necessary to get from A to B. Now her parents had taken over, arriving with smiles and practically carrying her out to their own car, a run-down Rover model which was all they could afford to run on their present income (though Keith had constantly advised them that a newer car would save them money in both fuel and maintenance, all things considered). Julia had tried to persuade them to take her car, the one she had used to get to work in the days when life had been normal and she had been well enough to go to work. Somehow she didn't feel it was likely that she would ever work again, even if she was going to live out her threescore years and ten.

Mum and Dad wanted her to stay at their house indefinitely, and part of her wanted to very much. To go back to being their child was about all she could bring herself to do at this point. It would be better for all concerned, they said, if she came back to live with them, and had her old room—the one in which she had spent her teenage years pining for Bryan Ferry, his life-size figure taking up almost the whole of one wall.

The poster was gone now, and the walls were no longer painted purple, but the smell of the past lingered. Julia remembered the evenings she had spent watching that view, listening to those familiar sounds—the railway in the distance, the occasional night bird. Her life had begun in those surroundings. Fitting if it ended the same way, but not yet. Her parents wanted her there so that they could keep an eye on her, and make sure she didn't "do anything silly". They didn't use those exact words, but she could almost hear them thinking them. In any case, they knew she would be too considerate to attempt suicide in their house.

On the first evening, the three of them sat together and watched a TV soap opera of which Julia's mother was fond. Later, after supper, her father suggested a game of cribbage, which he had taught Julia and Rebecca to play as children. He had to remind her of the rules. It was good for her, she knew, to concentrate on something like a card game, especially one with complicated rules and scoring. It took her mind away from the places it normally dwelled. Once the game was over and the cards and the board were put away—which was late—she realised how tired she was, and went to bed.

As she automatically got her nightdress out from under the pillow, where she knew her mother would have placed it, she was struck by the sudden shock of what had happened to her. It could have been twenty years before, she could have been young and innocent, unmarried and childless, in all except the important sense that she was none of these things. She was a married woman, with two children. It so happened, however, that they had been taken from her, and this was the reality she had to face. No amount of babying from her parents could erase that reality, and she knew, as she put her head down on the pillow with unshed tears, that she would spend no more than this one night in their house.

The following day, Julia moved back into her own home. Her parents only agreed to it when she swore to them, literally on the Bible, that she wouldn't repeat her suicide attempt. A health visitor was sent to call on her, a morose-looking woman of indeterminate age who clearly had only the vaguest idea of what it felt like not to want to live, her own intellect not being substantial enough to allow the possibility. She was used to talking to young mothers and their babies, and addressed Julia in similar fashion. There had been a certain amount of this kind of patronising rubbish in the hospital, but it was still an irritation.

After she had left, promising to call again, Julia broke down and sat for an hour sobbing, until interrupted by Edie Mayberry, the neighbour who had caused the police to break in and find her unconscious. Edie invited herself in, bringing her own biscuits as she knew that there "wouldn't be anything in the house". Her conversation was only moderately more bearable than that of the woman from the social services, though, to do her justice, she didn't attempt to remind Julia that she was the person who had saved her life. At least Edie had enough sense to know that her well-meaning action might not have met with the complete approval of the person it was intended to benefit. She steered clear of the subject altogether, talking to Julia as if she had just recovered from a serious illness—which in a manner of speaking she had—rather than the kind of devastating loss she had in fact suffered. The visit at least gave Julia a break from her own despair. She wasn't even obliged to join in the conversation, as Edie was happy to fill any prospective silence with the sound of her own voice. Having excused herself three times, on the grounds that Mr Mayberry would be wanting his dinner, she stayed for a further three-quarters of an hour, and even made another cup of tea. (She had come equipped with milk and sugar as well as the biscuits, "just in case".)

Becky phoned at about half-past six. She was tentative with her enquiries after her sister's health, and Julia knew exactly what was on her mind.

"It's all right, you know, you can mention the baby. I won't cry or anything like that." By now, she had become expert at disguising her voice to sound normal when the tears were rolling down her cheeks.

"I'm so sorry, Julia. I mean, I'm not sorry about the baby, I just wish it could all have been different. I wish it hadn't come at this time."

"If it hadn't, I'd be dead now."

"What?"

"Nothing." Julia didn't press it. Becky could do without being made to feel guilty for that as well.

They talked for an hour, touching on the experience of pregnancy but mainly keeping to safe subjects, such as Gordon's current job, and comparisons of the services offered by their local authorities. When Julia put the phone down, she felt better for a very short time. The anti-depressants the doctor had given her were very strong, much better than the ones she had been prescribed in the immediate aftermath of the accident. Already she was noticing a difference in her ability to cope with certain situations. Before going to bed, she made up her mind to re-decorate the living room.

A line had to be drawn under the last six months. Wallowing in grief was all very well while the prospect of your own death promised a finite period of suffering; but once you had crossed that boundary, and suicide had been discounted as an option, there was nothing to do but knuckle down to the task of living.

The capacity for rational thought, which had seemed to return to Julia slowly in the run-up to her overdose, and remained suspended afterwards somewhere in the region of her brain, was suggesting something to her. A key had to be found, which would let her back into the rest of her life. It might be a specific event or person, or an action that she needed to take. If she allowed herself the luxury of thought, it—the key to the future—might reveal itself.

It wasn't really a question of Julia allowing herself to think, so much as forcing her thought processes to function normally. Up to now, they had mainly been operating in reverse, looking back on things past, trying to re-write history. They needed to move forward—the wheels needed to turn in the opposite direction—so that she could seek something to make living worth while. The "key" she was looking for, whether or not it was an artificial device, was what would make them turn.

A week after she had come home from hospital, her resolve was already breaking. Becky's baby wasn't enough. It wasn't the key to Julia's future. It was only a reason for her not to die at this precise moment, not a reason for her to live. If she had been a different kind of person, she thought, she might have given herself over to charity work. Some people did, and it seemed to be enough for them. Just look at Mother Theresa.

A pointless comparison if ever there was one. Julia couldn't see herself working with the homeless. Giving them money was one thing, trying to hold a conversation with them quite another. In any case, most volunteer organisations would reject someone with her history, regarding her as too volatile, her suffering too fresh to enable her to be of use. Everything now depended on her own willpower. Decorating the house was a start.

The nightmares continued, naturally. Perhaps "nightmares" was not an accurate description, Julia thought when people asked her how she slept, but she couldn't think of any other way of explaining. They were dreams of longing, dreams in which the children—and, less often, Keith himself—were still alive. It had all been a mistake. They hadn't died. Or perhaps they had, but they had somehow been brought back to life and they were still with her and would always be. It was when she woke from these dreams that the real nightmare began.

In the morning, as usual, reality hit her with a blow in the guts as soon as she opened her eyes. There was no sound of cheerful banter and none of the general banging about as the boys pushed and shoved to be first in the bathroom. There was no sound of the electric kettle boiling and Keith whistling in the kitchen. There was no vestige of his warmth in the bed beside her. Emptiness reigned in the house.

Keith. All the things he was, and was not. All the times they had quarrelled, and shouted at one another in front of the boys. It was impossible to be sure whether she had loved him at the time of his death, though she was sure she had done at the time of their marriage. Regardless of what she felt or didn't feel for Keith, she would never have chosen anyone else to marry. Keith, whose body had been cut in half by the steering wheel of his car.

In those first few days back at home, Julia's parents called twice a day, once in the morning (to check that she hadn't killed herself during the night), and again in the evening (to check that she wasn't thinking of killing herself during the night). Her plans for decorating met with their enthusiastic approval. Aha, she mused, they think I've found a new interest in life. Her father took her to the D-I-Y superstore, where they toured the banks of emulsion and wallpaper while he gave an impromptu lecture on the importance of cleaning the paintwork thoroughly, preferably with sugar soap, prior to starting any re-decoration. He was clearly torn between wanting to do the job for her and wanting to see her carry through a task that would occupy her mind and her time.

The nature of her dreams was changing. Twice she dreamed that she was back in their old house, the one in Springfield Terrace. They had moved just before Andrew was born. In these dreams, she was another person, the young idealist. Keith didn't necessarily feature in such dreams, but neither did the children, as though she had gone back to a time before she had happiness, when everything was still in front of her—work, marriage, babies. This hankering after the past could take many forms, but it still had the same power to disrupt coherent thought. It was essential to keep going. Physical activity was the thing.

Some days later, Julia was alone in the house, up to her knees in newspaper, wearing an ancient overall she had inherited from her late Gran, when the doorbell rang. She assumed it was the postman, arriving late with a parcel. As she was walking to the door, she realised it couldn't be. Keith was no longer there to order books, and she hadn't needed any school uniform from her mail order catalogue this year. And never would again.

It was probably Mormons or Jehovah's Witnesses, or at the very least someone trying to sell brushes. Julia braced herself to be rude.

She sighed with relief as she realised she didn't need to be. Owen Richards looked apprehensive as he held out his hand, containing a coloured brochure, towards her.

"I hope I'm not disturbing you," he said, looking her up and down in that shrewd Welsh way of his. "I thought you might like to see the college prospectus for next year. You never know, there might be something…"

"Come in, Owen." She stood aside, not really thinking about why she was asking him in, just instinctively glad to see his face and hear his voice.

"I don't like to interrupt you, if you're busy," he said, in a tone that suggested a willingness to be very easily persuaded.

Once before, she remembered, she had drunk coffee with Owen. It had been a week or so before the exams, and she had been working in the computer lab one evening when he happened to be on duty. She had stayed late to finish her project, and he had offered her a hot drink before she drove home. They had sat in the store cupboard and talked about the exams, and then moved on to other things. She had been surprised to find that he read the same kind of books as she did, and liked the same kinds of music. He was the sort of person who, in other circumstances, she might have come to regard as a friend.

"Will you have a drink?" she asked, unthinkingly.

There was an awkward silence, during which Owen looked at his feet.

"I mean coffee," she said in exasperation. "I was just going to have one."

He came close to laughing with relief, then, as though realising that she couldn't take laughter, he converted it into a vigorous nod.

"Yeah, go on, you twisted my arm." She had forgotten how funny his accent could sound.

He was still awkward as he followed her into the kitchen.

"Doing some painting, then," he commented. "Need any help?"

"It's okay, I've had plenty of offers. My dad's just itching to see me make a mess of it, so he can take over."

"Just as well, really. I'm not very good at that kind of thing anyway."

She handed him a mug with "Sussex Archaeological Society" written on the side. It had been Keith's. She had found it in the back of the cupboard and brought it to the front. About time it was used again.

She didn't expect Owen to comment.

"Sussex Arch-aeo-log…Oh, I see. Is that one of your interests, then?"

"No, it was one of my husband's," she said, sounding curt in spite of herself.

Owen blushed. "Sorry," he said, in a faint voice.

"It's okay." She turned away so that he could not see how close she was to crying again. Today had gone so well up to now.

"Julia," came his voice from behind her, "if there was anything I could do. I mean, like, I know you don't know me that well, and I don't see you very often, but I hope…well, I really do mean it, you know. If there was anything I could do, you would ask me, wouldn't you?"

She nodded grimly, without turning round. "Yes, of course, Owen."

He was standing alongside her, holding out the prospectus again. "I've written my phone number on here. See?"

She was touched. "That's very kind of you."

He didn't stay long after that. It was too much to ask. But as he was going out of the front door, he repeated his offer of help. She knew that he genuinely wanted there to be something he could do for her. If only, she thought, there had been.

CHAPTER FIVE

When Julia had finished the living room, she considered redecorating the bedrooms. This was not a task she could stomach easily, but she had a vague idea that it would be a kind of therapy, the confronting of the horror that faced her. To step into the boys' bedrooms, to see their things still lying around where they had left them, and to set about the systematic demolition of her most happy and painful memories, so that she need no longer be haunted by them. It wouldn't work. She couldn't even go into Andrew's bedroom, so did it reek of his innocence. She knew that cobwebs hung there and that dust covered his treasured possessions.

Jeremy's room was different. He had been an unusually tidy boy, mature and thoughtful. He had put away all his things the night before he died, and as long as she did not look too closely at anything or open any of the drawers and cupboards, she could bear to walk about his room, remembering him, remembering the things that had not even happened yet, the degree ceremony, the wedding, the grandchildren, all the hopes she had had for her strong, bright, elder son.

To re-paint would no doubt have succeeded in erasing some of the memories, but it was too terrible a task to contemplate. The most she would be able to do was to get a little man in to do the job for her. She could perhaps give him a free rein, and tell him to take to Oxfam anything he found in the room that he did not want for his own family. Then, no doubt, she would regret what she had done. She could see herself running down to the shop to try to buy back a few small souvenirs of her boys, little plastic toys, coverless exercise books, things that had meant nothing to her while she still had their owners about the place.

For the present, Julia shelved the idea of touching the bedrooms. She still wasn't sure that she could remain in this house at all. Her opinion on that subject swung violently between a stubborn refusal to accept that anything had changed and a certainty that she couldn't bear to be in this familiar environment without the three other human beings who had made it "home".

Having completed the downstairs rooms, to her own and her father's satisfaction, she found time to sit down with the prospectus Owen Richards had given her and consider whether the college had anything to offer that might take her mind off her situation. There was an opportunity to learn Russian, on Tuesday evenings. By coincidence, that was the very evening she had been used to spending in class during her computing course. At school, she had been quite good at languages, but she had never kept up her French and German.

Russian was certainly a valuable language to know. If she turned out to be good at it, she could do a degree and get a job as a translator.

Julia knew that this was an idle fantasy, but it was fantasy—and lots of it—that she needed at this particular time, and the following morning she took a walk down to the college to see what she could arrange. She didn't need to go there in person, she could simply have telephoned, but the doctors had advised plenty of exercise and it took over half an hour to get there on foot.

There was an exhibition of paintings on in one of the lecture rooms. The main college building had changed quite a lot from how she remembered it. They had moved the main reception desk and carried out what is often fancifully called "refurbishment" of the public areas. The lecture rooms still looked rather dingy, though. As she had half-expected, there was no one available to enrol her properly on the course. She was simply told to "come along on the first night" and see whether she liked it. The course tutor was a Mr Steve Desborough.

It was a fortnight before the course would start, and Julia was hard pressed to find other things to occupy her mind in the meantime. Edie Mayberry helped her pass some of the intervening hours with her constant twittering, absorbed by Julia in the form of almost daily visits (usually on the pretext of "wondering if she needed anything from the shops"). Her parents, too, visited every day, though by the end of the second week they were down to a single visit a day, mainly because Julia had got into the habit of going out early in the morning to avoid their attentions. She would walk all over town, just as the shops were opening. Occasionally she would get on a bus, or even a train, and venture further afield, but she never got her own little car out of the garage, the car that had never been in an accident. It was almost new. She felt she ought to sell it, or give it away, but even that was too big a step to contemplate in her present state of mind.

Nora Penhaligon called once, just to see how she was getting on, and seemed to go away suitably reassured—though you could never tell with Nora. She didn't comment on the re-decorating, nor on the idea of a college course. One of the things Julia had come to like about Nora was the way that she never tried to reinforce other people's opinions or prejudices, nor even express any of her own. She was an intelligent woman, and perceptive enough to see that Julia meant to go on trying, regardless of the pain involved. That was her only concern, and when satisfied on that point, she left. Julia wished they could have met under different circumstances.

How different Nora was from Linda, despite the surface similarities. Linda called a couple of times, and sat stiffly in the kitchen, drinking coffee from a cup and saucer—Julia didn't dare offer her a mug. Linda didn't say much, because there was nothing she could say. Once she arrived when Edie was already there, and when Edie had at last left, smiling ingratiatingly and saying, "I'll leave you with your *friend* now," Linda's only comment was, "I don't know how you can tolerate that woman. Have you thought of moving?" Linda couldn't have meant it quite as it sounded. It was a reasonable comment, but it wasn't useful to Julia. She didn't encourage Linda to call again.

PJ rang sometimes from his office, the office he had shared with Keith, just to see how she was getting on. He had bought out Keith's share in the business at the earliest opportunity. He could afford it now, and the last thing he wanted was a sleeping partner. It gave Julia even more money, which she put into the building society and thought no more about.

For her, there were still the other times. Sometimes she would feel overcome when she was out at the shops—an activity she had always loved, which now held little pleasure for her. She avoided going into toyshops or shops that sold children's clothes, because they reminded her of the boys. She avoided bookshops and computer shops, because they made her think of Keith. Even the remaining shops held hazards—women out shopping with their children or their husbands, items for sale that carried unexpected memories of her lost family life. There was no getting away from it.

It was not usually these things that set her off, though. It was just the sheer pointlessness of it all. She could wander for hours with an empty mind, then return to the house and collapse sobbing on the floor at the sight of the newly painted living room. Nothing could ever restore her peace of mind. Even if someone could suddenly have given her a new, ready-made family identical to the last, it would not have been enough.

The decorating wasn't quite finished. Julia had an idea of re-tiling the kitchen, but knew it was over-ambitious. The last thing she wanted was to get halfway through a big job like that and find it was too much for her. It would be better to get someone in, right from the start. She looked in the yellow pages for someone local. There weren't many suitable entries under "Tiles", which mainly contained the names of places that sold tiles, with names such as Tile Tales, Tile Emporium and Tile Universe. Under "Painters and Decorators," there were some quarter-page adverts that claimed their sponsors could turn their hands to anything, including tiling. There was no answer from the first number she tried. The second had an answerphone service, and she left a message asking for someone to get back to her—without much hope that anyone would.

At the third attempt, she actually managed to speak to a human being (though, she felt afterwards, that was a loose description). George Holmes, self-proclaimed expert decorator, asked for details of the tiles she was planning to use and the square yardage she wanted tiled. Since she couldn't give a precise answer, he couldn't give an estimate and in any case he was booked solid for the next two months. "So what are you doing at home answering the phone?" she wondered, but made no comment, simply said thank you quickly, in a tone that told him what she thought of him, and slammed the phone down. Minor incidents like these were enough to upset her equilibrium for days on end, and she resolved not to let herself in for any more aggravation by pursuing the tiling idea.

On her way home from the shops next day, Julia took her customary shortcut, across a field behind suburban houses. Her mind on other things, she nevertheless noticed that the bushes were loaded with ripening blackberries. Waste was something she had always deplored, and later she took a plastic container and returned to divest the stalks of their blackest berries, with a view to making some kind of pie or crumble. It wasn't something she could eat on her own. Perhaps she would just stew a few for her own use, and give the rest to Edie.

She picked for two hours, finding it a soothing activity with a goal at the end of it that offered what would pass in her life for satisfaction. While picking, she thought of Owen Richards and his kindness, and wondered if she should invite him and his girlfriend, Jenny, round for dinner. The snag was that they knew all about her, and that would kill the evening stone dead. It would take a fourth person, preferably male, to make it work. Besides, Julia wasn't up to cooking an elaborate meal. She doubted whether she could even manage to open something ready-made and get it to look presentable.

After a bath, to take away the itchy feeling from being in the field and soak the juice stains off her hands and arms, Julia sought out a recipe involving blackberries. She found no shortage of such things, but all of them required an amount of effort and ingredients she didn't have. Stocks of even mundane things like flour and lard had been run down since the rest of the family died. Blackberries freeze well, advised a cookery magazine, one of the huge collection she had accumulated on a monthly basis throughout her married life but had rarely consulted. She put the berries in a freezer bag and shoved them in haphazardly. It was easier.

The calendar dragged itself feebly onwards to the beginning of the new college term, and Julia went to the library to see if there were any books that might help with her Russian course. The library held painful memories. It had been Keith's favourite place, and the boys had gone nearly every Saturday morning to change their books. They had both taken after their father and enjoyed reading. The regular assistant had known them all well, and carefully avoided any reference to Julia's personal situation, resulting in a strained and formal atmosphere which was only marginally preferable to the alternative.

At last, finally, the waiting ended and it was the first Tuesday night of the new term, time for Julia to try her hand at the Russian language. Steve Desborough turned out to be a thin, taciturn young man who knew his subject but had little talent for making it interesting to beginners. There was a break during the evening, when the students were able to go to the cafeteria and get a cup of coffee. Actually, the cafeteria was closed, but vending machines were available. The stuff they dispensed was hardly worthy of the name "coffee", but Julia found the hot chocolate tolerable, and forced herself to join three of the others from the Russian class at one of the formica-topped tables.

The conversation began with a man called Garfield introducing himself and asking the others "how they found the course". What he meant, of course, was what they thought of it so far, not how they found out that it existed. Julia was so entranced by the idea of anyone having such a ludicrous first name that she barely listened to what Garfield was saying. He was rather a pompous man, in his late fifties as she guessed. Probably divorced, she thought, realising with a sudden pang that in that case he was in much her own situation, separated from his loved ones, and probably suffering almost as much as she was. She had no right to make fun of such a man. The pomposity might only be his way of disguising the hurt and the feelings of worthlessness.

It was all speculation, anyway. Divorced or not, Garfield was hardly likely to discuss his private life with a group of people he had only just met for the first time. A quiet young woman called Gillian was speaking now. She already had a degree in French and Spanish, and worked as a librarian. She wore no wedding ring. The other person at the table was Mike, a man of about Julia's own age. He was one of those people who always seem to be smiling. Glancing across at Julia, he winked reassuringly. He appeared to find Garfield rather amusing. If he hadn't been almost completely bald, Mike would have been very attractive.

There were others in the class. A taxi-driver called Ian who was hoping to go on holiday to Russia, and expected to be able to converse with ordinary folk when he got there. (He was in for a disappointment, especially since he had displayed a total lack of linguistic aptitude in the first five minutes of the class.) A middle-aged teacher called Olive, and her husband, Neville, who never opened his mouth. An unemployed youth called Jason, who admitted he was only doing the course because it was free to the unwaged. And finally, a rather glamorous girl called Rowena, who appeared to have her eye on the tutor, Steve Desborough.

Although the class wasn't very interesting, Julia went home feeling pleasantly tired, and slept more easily than usual. Next day, she went to the nearest decent bookshop and bought or ordered the books Steve had recommended—all five of them. She could afford them, after all, and she might as well try and show some enthusiasm. In the evening, she was reading through her notes diligently when her parents arrived at the door, anxious to hear how her first Russian lesson had gone.

"Say something in Russian, then," coaxed her mother.

"Mum, we've only just started. I can't say anything yet."

Her mother's face fell. Her father, however, began to hold forth on the complexity of the Russian language. He had clearly been reading up on the subject in order to be able to encourage Julia's interest. In fact, he said, he was seriously thinking of taking up a language himself, as something to do in his retirement. What did Julia think? Would she recommend it as a hobby? Would she be willing to help him with his homework if he took up, say, German?

It was so tiring, having to pretend to be recovering.

CHAPTER SIX

Julia took her Russian studies seriously at first. Before the second class, she had assiduously gone over what little they had learned in that first two-hour session until she knew it off by heart. Now that she understood what the strange symbols of the Cyrillic alphabet stood for, she practised reading Russian words in the library, transliterating them and trying to make out whether they sounded familiar. The Russian word for an eating-place, for example, which she had always thought was "Pectopah," was in fact pronounced "Restoran". She could have guessed that it stood for "restaurant". There was some satisfaction to be gained from this exercise, but she had run out of steam several days before her second weekly visit to college.

After the library, she went to a small café that she had used to frequent before she was married. It had changed hands several times, and the ambience with it, but in fact she liked it better now, with its clientele of mainly middle-aged people, and it had become non-smoking, which was another plus. At the next table was a woman with two toddlers, a boy and a girl. Julia was tempted to get up and leave when they sat down, but forced herself to remain seated. In any case, it wouldn't have been easy to manoeuvre past the double buggy and the woman's shopping.

Watching the little boy run around in circles, ignoring his mother's repeated requests to "Sit down and be QUIET", Julia recalled with some guilt that she had often thought of her sons as handfuls. Though in general they had been well-behaved, more so than most of their friends, she had been ungrateful and had wanted more time to herself. Andrew, in particular, had gone through a phase of wanton destructiveness when he was about three. She had never meant to smack him, but nearly always ended up doing so.

The curly-haired little girl was sitting demurely at the next table, as little girls do. So different was she from what Julia remembered that she was able to look at her without the same feelings of loss and desperation. She had never regretted not having a daughter. She had thought them prissy, spoiled, affected little things. As a child, she had never been a girly girl. She had always looked like something the cat dragged in, dressed in dungarees, fingernails dirty, hair uncombed. Gradually, as she grew older, she had developed a kind of style. Money had helped. These days, she mostly slopped around in jeans and old jumpers, once again careless of her appearance.

The little girl she was watching was the serious type, intent on arranging the condiments that sat on the table, actually attempting to read the ketchup bottle, as children used to do in the times when there was nothing much else to occupy them. Knitting her little brows, she concentrated on her task, glancing with occasional contempt at her little brother who continued to run around the table noisily.

It was then that Julia knew she wanted another child.

Walking home afterwards, she started to think about it in earnest. If she had another child, not to replace what she had lost, but just to give her something to live for, she could stop being a burden to her parents. She wouldn't even have to envy Rebecca. She could live again. She wouldn't forget Jeremy and Andrew, or Keith, but she would have a reason to go on. What she needed was someone to need *her*.

She was forty-one. It was too old to think of starting another family. In all the months she had been receiving treatment and advice from others, no one had ever suggested it as a solution to her troubles. Even if she had been younger, she would still have needed to meet someone, go through the whole process of courting and so on, before they would be ready to have a baby together. She couldn't face all that. They surely wouldn't let her have artificial insemination, and she didn't have any of Keith's sperm frozen. Adoption was out of the question—her age would have been against her even if she hadn't been alone.

For a while now, Julia had stopped thinking about middle age. Once it had been a preoccupation, first for Keith, when he hit the big 4-0, and later for her, when she realised she wasn't far behind. Even though they had everything two people of their age group could want or expect from life, they pined for the past, for their "lost" youth and independence.

They had had it all. They hadn't missed out on much, when they were young. Julia had never been a gadabout, and neither, she knew, had Keith, but there had been parties, and learning to drink and smoke and swear and make love. She only did two of those things now—drink and swear—and she didn't even enjoy those. She had had it all, and now she had nothing. What was the point of being middle-aged, if you didn't have some reminder that you had once been young, and relatively happy? She needed something, if there was a way of getting it. Even Mum and Dad had salvaged something from their past.

What about Mum and Dad, anyhow? What would they say, what would they think? If the idea was to make them less anxious about her, it would be going the wrong way about it. They would be frantic with worry if she went in for a child at this stage in her life.

The pleasures of parenthood are overrated, she reasoned later. All that stuff about "giving life, the greatest gift". We do it all out of selfishness. Procreation, the desire to make yourself immortal, that's all it is. There's no logic to it. Human beings should know better.

Once formed, however, the idea wouldn't go away. Lying in bed at night, it returned to trouble her, pushing aside the usual tortured memories but not replacing them with any peace of mind. At breakfast the next morning, it was still there. *The sun comes up,*

I think about you… It reminded her of a song from a West End show she had seen with Keith. *The coffee cup, I think about you.* "Losing my mind", it was called. Appropriate, because that was precisely what she was doing.

It was now that Julia thought of using the telephone number that Nora Penhaligon had left with her. She had rejected the idea of "ongoing" counselling, determined as she was to wipe out the past few months, but maybe a chat with Nora was what she needed now. Nora might, just might, understand her feelings about another child.

The number had been put away carefully in a drawer. It hadn't been entered in the address book, which Julia didn't use or even look at any more. It contained the addresses and phone numbers of Keith's friends, Jeremy's friends, Andrew's friends. Perhaps one day Julia would buy a new address book, for the names and addresses of people that were part of her new life, which hadn't really started yet and perhaps never would. She could put the names and addresses of her Russian class in there perhaps, when she got to know them better.

Already, some of the class had dropped out. The unwaged young man did not appear for the second lesson, having had his money's worth. Olive's husband, Neville, was also missing. Clearly, he had only come to keep her company the first week, and, as she put it, "it wasn't what he was hoping". One wondered how a foreign language could be anything other than what it was. Julia was just thinking that she ought to go and sit by Olive, when Mike, the bald smiling man, arrived and slipped uninvited into the seat next to her.

"Hiya," he said, and winked again.

Julia wondered about him, whether he had taken a shine to her or whether he was always this way. Half of her wanted to believe that she could still be desirable to men. After all, if this wild scheme about another child was going to come to anything, she needed to find an admirer as soon as possible.

It was as well to have something to think about besides Russian, as Steve Desborough's teaching technique did not improve on closer examination. Julia thought she had seldom seen a less attractive man, so lacking in personality. What made Mike, the smiling man, attractive was precisely that, his personality. She doubted that *he* ever had difficulty finding women, baldness notwithstanding.

The time before the coffee break seemed endless. In the cafeteria, much as she had expected, Mike placed himself next to her at the table. He was the centre of the group, talking, laughing, but there was little doubt that he had a particular interest in her. She began to hope that he was not married.

A good way of finding out whether a man is married, as she had found out in the past, is to ask them if they have any children. Dropping in a mention of "your wife" is too obvious, but the question about children is okay for some reason. If they are single, they usually look shocked, laugh and reply, "Me? No, I'm not married." The problem with this approach, for Julia, was that it required to be introduced by a comment or anecdote about children. She could hardly begin by saying, "Both my children were killed in a car crash", nor could she easily pretend and talk about them in general conversation as if they were still living.

Mike saved her the effort by working "my ex-wife" into the conversation after only a few minutes. She knew, with an awful certainty, that the sole purpose of the remark was to let her know that he was available. He had sensed something about her, she knew. She hadn't thought she was giving off such clear signals.

Now that she had engineered the opportunity, Julia found herself unable to respond, but made desperate attempts at small talk of a non-flirtatious (or so she hoped) nature until it was time to return to the classroom. At least Mike didn't offer her a lift home. It would have been very hard to know what to do. She didn't want to appear stand-offish by refusing, but she had always known that she wasn't a particularly good judge of character, at least on first acquaintance. She often liked people the first time she met them and only discovered later that they were full of flaws; whereas other people, whom she took an immediate dislike to, later became firm friends. For example, she had been quite wrong in her assessment of

Garfield's background. He was happily married; it was just that his wife wasn't interested in learning Russian.

The possibility of inviting Mike to dinner along with Owen Richards and Jenny—Julia didn't even know her surname—came into her mind. He would be the ideal guest, witty and good-humoured. Furthermore, he didn't know about her past, so he wouldn't have to bite his tongue and avoid referring to it. Yes, but Owen and Jenny *did* know, and that would be sure to spoil the atmosphere. Would they have anything in common, anyway? She couldn't really picture Owen and Mike sharing a joke or comparing football teams.

As she was leaving the building, she glanced into one of the few rooms that was still lit, and saw Owen, of all people, poring over a computer listing at an empty desk beside a terminal. At that precise moment, he looked up and saw her. Quickly, he rose and came to the door.

"Julia," was all he said, but he didn't look displeased to see her.

"Hello, Owen." She looked around her nervously. "As you see, I took your advice about doing a course."

"That's great. What are you doing?"

"Russian."

"Oh." He faked an expression of awe. "Intellectual."

"No, but difficult. Which is what I need."

He turned sideways, opening a path into the room. "Come in and have a coffee?" he suggested.

"Aren't you busy?"

"No. I was about to knock off, actually. I hadn't noticed the time."

"I shouldn't hang around, really. I don't like walking home in the dark."

"I could give you a lift."

She sized up the offer. She had scarcely been in a car since the accident, but she had known she was going to have to break the habit sooner or later.

"I don't know, Owen. If you can understand, I don't travel by car much these days. It's nothing personal."

"Course not." He slapped his forehead, sending ginger-blond hair flapping. "My stupid fault for not thinking." He hesitated. "I suppose buses are just as bad, are they?"

Forgetting herself for a moment, she laughed. The act of laughter, though she rarely indulged in it, always made her feel worse. She had no right to do it. She looked around the room. There were a couple of computer terminals, a couple of desks, a couple of tatty chairs, and nothing much else.

"Is this your office?" she enquired.

"Not exactly. I haven't got an office, but there's a staff room. That's a bit more comfortable, if you want to go in there."

"No, I don't really. I need to go home now. Is the offer of a lift still on?"

"Yeah, course. Just let me switch everything off, and I'll be with you."

Julia watched as he went around the room disconnecting things and sweeping the computer listing into a desk drawer. A simple life, it looked. She wondered vaguely whether there was any chance of her getting a job at the college. A job might be what she needed to take her mind off the necessity of living; but it seemed obscene to take one when she was so comfortably off. Charity shops had been suggested, but she didn't think she could stand that for long.

"Right, then," said Owen, breaking in on her train of thought. "My car's up the road, I'm afraid. Actually, it's Jenny's car, not mine. I couldn't get in the staff spaces today. It's not far, though."

Together they left the building, crossed the road and walked about fifty yards to where an elderly red Fiat stood in splendid isolation. These roads around the college were always full of parked cars on a weekday morning, but at night it was quiet as a graveyard.

It was raining lightly. Julia put up the hood of her coat. Owen, bareheaded, seemed untroubled by it. They walked in silence. Owen opened the passenger door with the key before going round to the driver's side. Julia had always hated the way that Keith used to get in the car first, before reaching over to unlock the passenger side for whoever was with him. That was in the days before they could afford a car with central locking, of course.

Why did Owen always make her think of Keith?

Owen, who, Julia suspected, was cautious by nature, appeared to be making a conscious effort to drive carefully, as they wound their way through the dark, wet streets. He made a brief attempt at friendly conversation, but it was difficult to make small talk without getting onto the subject of families.

A rash thought struck her as the Fiat came to a rattling halt outside her front door.

"I don't suppose you'd like to have my car."

She couldn't see Owen's face clearly, but his apprehension was almost tangible.

"What? What do you mean? You want to sell it?"

"No, I want to give it to you."

He laughed nervously, thinking it was some kind of wild joke from an unhinged woman. She had meant it, but she felt, as she put the key into the front door, that it would be unwise to mention it again.

"Will you come in and have a drink?"

He didn't refuse, as she had feared. He might think she was mad, but he probably felt sorry for her rather than afraid of what she might do or say next.

They went into the kitchen. Owen sat quietly on a stool while Julia made the coffee. He might be nervous of her, but he showed no sign of agitation. The gracefulness of his body struck her, in the way he dangled his long legs in front of him while they waited for the kettle to boil. If Keith had done that, she would have told him to get his big feet out of her way, but she felt indulgent towards Owen.

His jeans were too short, she noticed, and an inch or so of white flesh showed above the tops of his black socks.

"How's the decorating going?" he asked at last, as she handed him his drink.

"I've stopped for the time being. I did the living room and the study, and the hall and the landing, as you can see, but I can't face the boys' bedrooms." It slipped out easily, she was pleased to note. Some days she couldn't get the words out.

He stared into his mug.

"I could do a bit for you, if you like."

He could hardly have looked less comfortable with his own suggestion if he had tried.

"That's awfully kind of you, but I'm just not ready to have those rooms disturbed. I think I'll get someone to come in and give them a good clean before I do anything with them. Maybe I'll get the Salvation Army or someone to come and clear out all the stuff. I can't even look…"

It was essential to stop at this point if she didn't want to start crying. Fortunately, Owen was sensitive to the danger. He didn't want to see her cry, any more than she wanted to cry in front of him.

"Say no more. But don't forget, if there ever *is* anything I can do, I'll be only too glad to oblige. Don't ever be afraid to ask, okay?"

He meant it, in his way. They all did, all those people who offered help, though Owen seemed to be more persistent than most.

She dreamed about him that night.

CHAPTER SEVEN

It was the kind of dream she hadn't had for a few years, certainly not the kind she had had in recent months, since the accident. It was the kind of dream she occasionally used to have during her marriage, about other men, usually men she worked with, the kind of dream that made her feel slightly discontented with Keith. Lovable as he was in many ways, he had irritating habits. He was not the man she had married. He had grown overweight, he was difficult to please, and she no longer found his forgetfulness endearing.

In the dream, she was with Owen, and they were intimate. Not having sex, or even kissing, just leaning their heads against one another and talking in quiet voices, feeling content and satisfied. At last they were together, as it was meant to be.

It was that morning that Julia started to think seriously about what Owen had said the night before. There *was* something he could do, after all. He could be the father of her child.

She had been assuming that she would seek out someone she didn't know before, strike up a relationship with them, and use the sex between them, which everyone expected these days, as the means to get a child. That had always been fraught with difficulty, because supposing she didn't get pregnant, she might find herself stuck with someone she wasn't that bothered about.

A one-off would have been the alternative, but once again she had been assuming that it would be with someone she hadn't known before, a spur-of-the-moment thing after a night out. Perhaps she wouldn't even know his name, and he would certainly not know that she was pregnant by him when it happened. There were all kinds of problems with that approach too. The child might inherit the genes of someone who was unhealthy or just plain not nice— a criminal, even. A casual pick-up might also insist on taking precautions. People were so frightened of getting AIDS or, worse still, getting caught by the Child Support Agency.

Now that the idea of getting Owen to do it had implanted itself in her mind, Julia was astonished that she had not thought of it sooner. Owen was so obvious. She had always liked him— well, almost always. She had always been attracted to him. She knew he liked her as a friend, and she didn't think he found her physically repulsive. He seemed quite—dare she think it?—fond of her. The best thing of all about him was that he was so different from Keith.

She put the thought to one side. The whole idea of another child was "off the wall", as Keith would have said.

In all the time she had been without him, Julia had never once felt that Keith was near her, looking down on her from heaven or wherever the dead go, watching over her from the afterlife, protecting her, a guardian angel, a spirit. Nor had she ever felt any awareness of the boys continuing to exist as spirits or souls. It had destroyed her belief in life after death.

If she had still believed, as she used to believe, then death would have been a welcome thought. It was welcome, but only because Julia could no longer face living. Living without the boys was intolerable. She could have lived without Keith. Honesty was essential in that quarter. But she couldn't live without her children. There wasn't any point.

When she got up in the mornings, she always felt cold. Keith had always given off heat in bed. It was an odd thing for someone who seemed to expend as little energy as he did. Men were always warm, though. Female acquaintances had confirmed that. It was the women who had cold feet, which they planted on their husbands in bed to warm up.

In that respect, she missed Keith a lot.

Impossible to go on like this. It was time to telephone Nora Penhaligon.

The scrap of paper with the number on it was brought out of the drawer. Tentatively, Julia picked up the receiver and dialled. The number was engaged. Maybe later.

The week was going by slowly. There was nothing much to look forward to except Russian class, and the possibility of seeing Owen again. Julia knew that she ought not to think about him, but somehow he kept creeping into her psyche. What on earth would he have thought if he could have seen inside her mind?

On Wednesday, Rebecca phoned to say that she was coming down to visit at the weekend. It was totally unexpected. Julia didn't know how to face her. Telephone conversations were superficial, not the same as seeing someone. She hadn't actually seen Becky since just before the suicide attempt, and now so much had changed that she was afraid of seeing her. Guilt, she supposed it was, that she should be a blight on Becky and Gordon's happiness at this time.

There had never been many close female friends for either of the two sisters. They could talk to one another in a way they couldn't with anyone else. So much shared experience, so many memories. Julia had always tried to be there for Becky, and Becky, though she was younger, had reciprocated. It had been hard when Becky and Gordon moved away. They had written and phoned one another regularly. In latter times, Keith had urged Becky to get connected up to the Internet, so that they could communicate by e-mail.

Putting down the telephone receiver after Becky's call, Julia thought of ringing Nora again. It was after six, so she probably wouldn't be there—or was it her home number she had given Julia? Surely not. If Nora had given an out-of-hours number, then it must be for use in emergencies.

Was this an emergency?

Julia didn't want to talk to Nora on the telephone in any case. She only wanted to arrange a visit, or a face-to-face meeting. She dialled. After three or four rings, an answerphone clicked in. Not another of those infernal machines. It wasn't Nora's voice either, but an official-sounding woman who asked her to leave a message and "someone will get back to you".

"I want to speak to Nora Penhaligon," she said after the tone, noting the shakiness in her own voice. "It's Julia Grant. I want to speak to Nora. If possible. Some time. She's got my number."

As she put down the receiver, she realised that it was unreasonable to think that Nora would have her number to hand. It would be filed away somewhere in her office, with the telephone numbers of other insane women, probably men too. Would Nora even be able to remember her?

She expected a return call the following morning, but it was late afternoon before it came. It wasn't Nora either.

"Mizz Grant?" asked the voice. Julia's skin prickled.

"Speaking."

"You left a message last night, for Nora Penhaligon?"

"Yes, that's right."

"I'm afraid Mrs Penhaligon's not available. My name's Danielle Hunt. I wonder if you'd like to talk to me instead."

"Er...no. I mean, nothing personal, but I'd rather talk to Nora. When will she be available?"

"Sorry, I should have explained. Nora's not with us any more."

Not with us? An irrational thought expressed itself without waiting for the brain's logic circuits to catch up with it.

"You mean she's dead?"

There was an awful silence.

"No." Danielle Hunt laughed nervously. "No, nothing like that. Nora's been transferred to another office."

"Oh." Julia could only think how stupid she must have sounded. "I'm sorry, I thought...I mean, of course...You couldn't get in touch with her, could you?"

"Well..." Danielle Hunt wasn't going to say yes, but didn't want to say no. How could one syllable express so much? "It's not normal procedure. If it was an emergency, and no one else could deal with it, we might consider that, but really, unless it was something really serious… I can assure you that I'm a trained counsellor, and I know all about your case—all about you, I mean. I'd be only too pleased to call on you, if you'd prefer to talk in person. I could call tomorrow, if you like. Can you give me some idea what it's about, or is it just a general chat you want?"

This wasn't going to work. Julia could feel her powers of resistance ebbing away.

"Um. It's general, really, but there's a specific problem I wanted to talk about. To ask advice. I'm not sure you'd understand. I don't want to talk about it on the phone."

"Of course, I quite understand that. Why don't we arrange for me to call tomorrow?"

"No, not tomorrow. I've got my sister coming for the weekend. Another day."

"Monday then? I've got meetings in the morning, but I could come in the afternoon. Or Tuesday?"

"Monday's fine. Thank you." There was no point in arguing.

Becky's face looked thin, despite the now noticeable bump under her dress. She didn't look particularly well, in fact. Julia forgot her own troubles momentarily.

"If you don't mind me saying so, you look a bit peaky. Are you okay?"

"Honestly, Jules, I had no idea how hard this was going to be. I didn't want to come clean with Mum and Dad, but I don't mind telling you. Some mornings I've felt unbelievably awful. I'm putting on weight very slowly, they say—although I feel massive."

"It's normal." Julia pulled herself up short to prevent herself launching into reminiscences of her own experience.

"I hope you're not angry with me for not telling you. About the baby, I mean. I never told a soul, except Gordon. And the doctor, of course. I was so scared that something would go wrong."

"I can understand that. Don't worry, I'm not offended."

"But I keep thinking, if I'd told you...Would it have made any difference?"

"Probably not," Julia lied.

"Are you over it now? Sorry, I don't mean that. I mean, are you still feeling suicidal?"

"No." She didn't want to add that she had given up contemplating suicide for the moment only because of Becky's pregnancy. That was too much responsibility for a person to bear.

"Let's go out to lunch," said Julia, in an effort to get away from the subject of children.

"I'm afraid I wouldn't be very good company. I can't eat much. I get morning sickness all day, then I get heartburn if I eat a large meal. Even a medium-sized meal, actually. I just snack all the time. It's the only way."

"Okay, then let's go to the café down the road and have a sandwich." Julia suggested this place only because she knew it was licensed. She had to have a drink.

A little later, with wine inside her, she had begun to feel a little better, though she wasn't supposed to touch alcohol while on this course of tablets. Fortunately, Becky didn't ask. Becky, of course, didn't drink now.

"Dad says you're learning Russian," Becky commented between mouthfuls of a salad sandwich. "It must be really difficult."

"Mmm." Julia realised she was not making enough effort to seem in good spirits. "Yes, it is hard, but it's good fun. I've made some friends in the class." It was a lie, but in a good cause. This week's class had been enjoyable though, insofar as she was capable of enjoyment. She hadn't seen Owen, but he had dropped a note through the door one day when she was out, just saying that he had called on the off-chance and hoped she was okay. She had been so upset at having missed him that she had cried all afternoon.

"Do you think you might take it further?" Becky broke into her drifting thoughts again.

"Don't know about that. I can barely string two words together as yet. Ask me in a year's time."

They laughed together, but Becky's laughter was uncomfortable, and Julia's forced.

"How did you get interested in it?"

"Someone gave me a brochure." All of a sudden, she relished the opportunity to talk about Owen. "Someone I knew when I was doing that computing course. Do you remember that?"

Becky nodded, smiling, clearly pleased that Julia was opening up.

"He used to work in the computer lab, but now he's a lecturer. It was very thoughtful of him. He even brought the brochure round to the house."

"You know him quite well then?" asked Becky, cautious in her approval.

"We used to be quite friendly. But I hadn't seen him for ages. He'd heard…you know, and he came to visit me in hospital."

"Oh!" Becky covered her surprise well. "That was nice of him."

Julia knew what she was thinking. She had been too extravagant in her praise of Owen. Becky was wondering why Mum and Dad hadn't mentioned this paragon who was taking an interest in Julia.

"He's only a young lad," she exaggerated. "I know his girlfriend too." It was so easy to lie once you got started, or to bend the truth. She had been doing it ever since the accident.

Rebecca could only stay for the weekend, but it was nice to have the house seeming lived in again. She slept in the spare room, the only one Julia could use for visitors. Becky was the first visitor she had had in months. They talked about old times, skilfully avoiding the subjects that caused most distress. It was easy enough, Julia found, to talk about Keith and things that he had said and done in the distant past, but not so easy to refer to any incident involving the children. She convinced herself that it was for Becky's benefit.

CHAPTER EIGHT

After Becky had gone, Julia found herself coming back to the subject of Owen fathering her child, and pondered on it further. This was getting ridiculous. Not only was she obsessed with this wild idea of having another child, but she was starting to convince herself that there was only one man who could give her what she wanted. Why couldn't she find someone more suitable? Someone who at least wasn't attached. Logically, though, that might be a drawback, because a single man might want to have more to do with the child than Julia herself cared to give him. She didn't want to live with another man, not yet. She just wanted a child to lavish her attention on.

It would be dangerous, giving all that love and affection to one child. It would make Julia even more obsessive than she already was, especially in terms of the child's safety. She would constantly worry that he or she was going to be snatched away from her as the boys had been. That desperation would pass itself on to the child, subconsciously, and it would end up spoiled, petulant and self-centred, especially if there was no father to dilute the effect.

She recalled how she had doted on Jeremy in the early months and years, how she had eventually forced Keith to agree to having a second child simply because she was so afraid of her feelings. As the years passed, the obsession grew weaker if it never altogether faded away, though she felt the familiar pangs when Andrew was small. The older the children became, the more their personalities developed, the more differently they grew from how she had expected, the less she thought about them. By the end of their lives, they had become part of the wallpaper. It should have made it easier to live without them, but somehow it hadn't turned out like that.

Could Julia guarantee that she wouldn't waste another opportunity of motherhood as she now felt she had wasted the first two?

There was no solution.

By Monday afternoon, Julia had almost forgotten about Danielle Hunt's visit. It was only at the moment the doorbell rang that she realised who it must be.

The woman who stood on the doorstep was younger than Nora, and prettier.

"Julia? I'm Danielle. We spoke on the phone."

Her voice was softer than it had sounded over the wire. She didn't quite have Nora's air of confidence.

"Come in, please."

Danielle accepted the offer of coffee. It was all part of the training, Julia knew. If the client wants to busy herself making coffee, let her. Put her at her ease. Only in this case it was probably Danielle who needed putting at her ease, because she couldn't disguise her anxiety. Julia resisted the temptation to ask how new Danielle was at the job. It didn't matter anyway.

"So, Julia, how have you been getting on since Nora saw you in—September, wasn't it?"

"Not so badly. I go from day to day, if you know what I mean." No sense in making Danielle more uneasy, at least not at this stage.

"I hope you'll understand that we've kept notes on you, and I've had to consult them. They're kept completely confidential, and we don't look at them unless there's a reason to. Then, after a while, we destroy them."

After five or ten years, probably.

"That's okay," said Julia. "I can understand that. You've got a job to do, after all."

"And are you feeling all right, physically?"

"Yes, generally okay. I'm still on the anti-depressants, of course."

"Of course, yes. And are you working again?"

"No, I couldn't face that. Well, I could face it if I could find the right job, but that's not likely, and anyway, I don't need the money."

"No, but perhaps you need something to occupy you. Nora said—in the notes—that you were thinking of taking up a hobby."

Julia couldn't now remember if she had told Nora about the Russian classes.

"I go to an evening class. I'm learning Russian."

"Russian? Great! I'd love to learn Russian, but I'm not very good at languages. Is it very difficult?"

All these practised moves. Make conversation. Draw the client out. Danielle was much more obvious than Nora had ever been.

"Quite difficult, yes. But mentally stimulating."

"And have you made any new friends?"

Bad move, Danielle. Making the client feel like a social outcast.

"One or two." Julia didn't really feel it was a lie.

"Great!"

There was a hiatus in the conversation. Julia could see Danielle mentally accessing her training material for the next ploy. She felt obliged to help her out.

"There was something I wanted to talk about. I don't know whether you'll understand."

She already knew that Danielle wouldn't understand, but it was probably worth talking about it, just to see how it sounded when she said the words.

"Try me." Danielle was eager, for obvious reasons. She would be able to relax a little while Julia was talking.

"It's like this, you see. I don't know if you've got any children of your own." She didn't pause for a reply. It didn't matter anyway. "It's a physical urge, to have children, as well as an emotional one. I had children—as you know. When I had them, I sometimes wondered if I had any right to them. I mean, when you're in hospital, everybody refers to it as 'your' baby, they even put labels on it to make sure you get the right one."

She paused long enough to notice that Danielle was looking increasingly blank.

"But really, when it comes down to it, what gives you the right to that child? It's only a convention that the women who actually give birth are the mothers of the children, and the men whose sperm has been used are the fathers. There's nothing else that gives you the right. You might not even want that child. I mean, look at my sister, she always wanted a child, longed for one. I wasn't that bothered in the beginning, but it was easy for me to get pregnant. What gave me the right to have them, more than her?"

Little frown lines were beginning to crease Danielle's forehead.

"And *yet*, when you've got them, and they're yours, and no one can take them away from you—or so it seems—you love them. And you want them, and you feel so much for them, and it's even more than your instinct for self-preservation. You'd gladly die for them. I would have died a hundred times over if my children could have survived that car crash."

Julia's eyes were beginning to moisten, but for once she didn't feel as embarrassed as Danielle looked. Oh, to hell with Danielle, surely she must have seen this kind of thing before.

"Then, suddenly, you're without them, and you realise you never did have any right to them after all. And maybe you did something wrong, maybe you didn't look after them properly, because as they get older, they start to become people instead of children, and you can't control them, you haven't got any power over their thoughts or their actions. *Anyway…*"

She thought it might be better not to look at Danielle at all.

"…the thing that's bothering me is—you might not understand this—the thought that I'm not quite old enough to be unable to get pregnant again. I *could*, I could have another child. I'm not sure how I would go about it, but I could, theoretically anyway, I could do it. And I have this feeling that it would be the answer to all my problems. But then I think, even if I could do it, would I be any better at looking after it than I was with my other…with my sons? Would it just be a stupid thing to do, would it be unfair on the child? Do you understand?"

Danielle didn't understand. Julia could tell just by looking at her. It was unfair to expect it. She probably didn't even have kids of her own. Nora might have understood, but Danielle clearly didn't.

"Gosh, Julia," she said at last. "That's a very difficult question, you know—whether it would be the right thing for you. And I can't answer it. Have you got a...hmm, boyfriend?"

Julia shook her head and looked down. She hadn't expected such a ridiculous question, even from a social worker. Now she was going to have to sit through some pointless discussion between Danielle and Danielle, with herself possibly supplying the words that she thought Danielle wanted to hear. She looked into the middle distance, her gaze lighting suddenly on a threadbare patch just below the arm of the settee. How could it have got like that? Julia only caught bits of what followed.

"If you were in a relationship, then of course it would be great ...think about yourself...not feel guilty...hurt and guilty...problems of looking after a child...feeling alone...support."

Eventually there was a need for Julia to get out of the chair, and, more importantly, to get Danielle out of the house.

"Thanks, Danielle, you've been a great help."

Danielle looked surprised. "I don't know if I've said anything really helpful."

"Oh, yes, of course, you have. I knew it was a silly idea, really, I just needed to talk it through with someone."

"I hope you understand, Julia, I wouldn't dream of judging you."

"Of course not. I understand. Thanks for coming, really."

"Would you like me to call again?"

Oh God, no. Now it would never end.

"I don't think that'll be necessary, thanks. You've helped me clarify my thoughts."

"Well, you've got my number. If you ever need to talk..."

"Yes, yes, I'll remember that. Thanks again."

She resisted the urge to push Danielle bodily through the front door. She needed to seem calm and decided, otherwise the girl certainly would call again, whether requested to or not. But it wouldn't matter if she called a hundred times, Julia could still never have told her about Owen.

Nora, she thought, how could you let me down like this, when I really did need you?

CHAPTER NINE

The next Russian lesson was drawing closer. Julia found herself counting the hours until she would—possibly—have another opportunity to talk to Owen. Determined not to go out of her way to see him, she nevertheless hoped that their paths might cross. It wasn't terribly likely. He didn't work late every evening. The other week had been a one-off; he had said so himself.

All the same, she was disappointed when she walked past the office where she had seen him previously and found it dark and empty. Mike was walking with her, having latched on to her unexpectedly at the end of the class. He didn't waste any time.

"How are you getting home, Julia?"

She considered explaining to him the reasons why she didn't drive or accept lifts, but it was too much hassle. She knew what would happen—his expression would change to one of barely concealed horror, and by the following week, everyone in class would know her situation and be falling over themselves not to mention marriage or children in her presence. It was such a relief sometimes to be in the company of people who weren't sensitive to her personal history that she didn't want to put it in jeopardy.

"I walk. It's not far."

"Oh, you mustn't do that. Isn't there anyone who can collect you?"

This was difficult. Soon she was going to be forced to give something away.

"No, I haven't got anyone. I live on my own."

That ought to be enough. How Mike chose to interpret it was up to him.

"In *that* case, I'll give you a lift." The way he put it, she could hardly refuse without offence. She thought, as they walked towards a rather flashy black model, that it was true about men resembling their cars. Mike was nice, but with a trashiness about him that she had seen through early on. She already knew, before he turned on the ignition, that his driving would be skilful, but not careful.

During the short drive, they chatted about the class. Mike had already ascertained the major facts worth knowing about most of the other students as well as the lecturer. He knew Steve Desborough's age and academic record, as well as his family background. Julia was at a loss to understand how he had managed to find out so much without having made any obvious attempt to pal up with Steve. It was unusual for a man to take such an interest in others, and especially ironic in view of how little he knew about Julia, who probably, she thought without pleasure, had the most interesting life story of anyone in the class. But then, what he told her about Steve might not have been true. Perhaps he was inferring a lot of it.

"How do you know so much about Steve?" she asked outright. He didn't seem to mind the question.

"I know a lot of the lecturers here. One of my best mates used to work here, in the computer lab."

Julia gulped.

"Do you…Do you know someone called Owen Richards?"

Mike didn't react. "Don't think so. What's he look like?"

"Red hair. Mid-thirties. Tall, slim."

"I think I know who you mean. Don't think I've ever spoken to him though. Friend of yours?"

"I used to know him. I did a computing course here a few years ago."

That opened up new avenues of conversation, which lasted until they arrived at Julia's door. To her relief, Mike didn't switch off the engine and didn't appear to expect to be asked in. Either he wasn't interested after all, or he knew better than to come on too strong straight away. Playing hard to get, she thought, and almost smiled.

"Thanks very much," she said pointedly. "See you next week."

She turned round to wave from the doorway. He had, naturally, waited to see her safely in, then he sounded the horn unnecessarily and drove off noisily. Edie wouldn't approve, thought Julia.

The house always felt so cold now, even when the central heating had been on. Julia had got into the habit of turning on the television or radio before she went out, to give the illusion of someone in the house—not for the benefit of would-be burglars, but simply to make the place feel lived in.

The weather forecast was just finishing. It wasn't good. Autumn was well and truly setting in. Soon there would be Christmas—the shops were already preparing for it. Decorations were everywhere. The previous Christmas there had been a big debate over whether to buy Andrew a mountain bike as his main present. The bike lay in the garage now. He had used it perhaps twice before the accident. He had been waiting for the finer weather.

CHAPTER TEN

It was the thought of Christmas that finally decided Julia. She couldn't go on like this, she couldn't face Christmas unless she had something to think about, the possibility that she might be pregnant. It was selfish, but she could see no other way. If she didn't do it now, before she turned forty-two and started thinking about the menopause, she would make this, and every other Christmas, a misery for the rest of the family.

Visits to the supermarket were infrequent now. When Julia did go, she stocked up with a few weeks' worth of individual freezer meals and tinned goods—the small tins, of course. Sometimes, just sometimes, she would find herself reaching for something the boys had liked—potato crisps or chocolate flavour breakfast cereal—before snatching her hand back at the sudden realisation that she no longer had to cater for them. There was still food in the house, jars of peanut butter and tins of spaghetti hoops, which she didn't eat herself and couldn't bear to throw away. She was waiting for one of those charities that sometimes appeal for things to put in food parcels destined for some foreign war or famine zone. Probably, at Christmas, a crisis charity would be glad of donations of food for the homeless. Maybe she could go and help serve Christmas dinner to tramps in some hostel or other.

Shopping for one wasn't enjoyable, even though she was now able to buy the things she liked to eat without wondering whether there would be an opportunity to use them. Butter beans, for example. Keith had hated them, the boys had hated them, but Julia had always liked them. She could have them for every meal now, if she cared to, but there was no satisfaction in that. Once she had loved food, but now it held no interest for her. Red meat, in particular, couldn't be touched unless it was in some totally unrecognisable form, like the filling of a Cornish pasty. For a time, she had virtually lived on green salads, the tasteless crunch of the lettuce reassuring her that she was taking in some form of nourishment whilst not enjoying it—a kind of penance. There were other problems with shopping too. So many times Julia had been tempted to buy a dozen eggs or a multi-pack of something, and then, perhaps much later on, remembering that she couldn't use them, had put them back on the shelf, looking around in embarrassment in case anyone was watching her.

Today, as she approached the checkout, she noticed a handwritten sign, reading, "Part-time temporary vacancies to cover Chrismas period. Please ask for an application form." She wondered what kind of person wouldn't be able to spell "Christmas". Someone who wasn't a Christian, presumably. As the teenage boy behind the checkout desk began to scan her goods, she blurted impulsively, "Could I have an application form, please?"

His blank look made her realise she had been too ambitious. "I saw a sign over there," she explained, "saying that there are vacancies—jobs—in the run-up to Christmas. Where do I get an application form?"

The boy paused to consider the question. It had always annoyed Julia that checkout assistants had to stop everything else they were doing when called on to speak, as though it were too much for their little brains to cope with, talking and thinking at the same time.

"You'll have to ask at Customer Services," he said, and pointed vaguely.

It wasn't difficult to find the Customer Services desk, near the entrance to the shop, but the assistant on duty was not much more helpful. "I don't know if we've got any," she said slowly, as though she expected Julia simply to give up and go away. Then she called an older woman, a supervisor. They talked for a few moments, too quietly for Julia to hear. There were hand gestures, and eventually a form was produced from under the counter.

"You've got to fill this in, dear," said the supervisor, taking over, "and hand it in to Personnel."

"Where is that, please?" asked Julia.

"Well, you can hand it in here, if you like," said the woman.

Julia took the application form into the supermarket coffee shop, which was fortunately very quiet, to look it over. Depositing her bags by the nearest table, she got herself a cappuccino out of the self-service dispenser, paid for it, and sat down with the form. It was poorly laid out, but there was no information required that she didn't have to hand. Even her National Insurance number was written in her diary, which was in her handbag.

She handed in the form, and asked how long it would be before she heard anything.

"I don't think we're taking on anybody at the moment," said the assistant on duty, now someone completely different from those she had spoken to fifteen minutes earlier.

"But the sign says…"

"It's an old sign," sighed the assistant. She pondered. "I suppose I should get somebody to take it down."

Julia felt the tears rising into her eyes, and her voice trembled as she said sharply, "Maybe next time you put one up, you can try and spell 'Christmas' correctly."

She stormed out of the supermarket, buffeting other shoppers with her bags, and walked home in a fury, face red and tears streaming.

Why was God doing this to her?

By the time she got home, she felt slightly calmer. She would get her own back on the supermarket by never going there again. That would teach them a lesson. Perhaps she would write a letter of complaint. The head office, wherever it was, was bound to be apologetic. She remembered an occasion when Keith, in a chain store, had been drawn into an argument with the manager and had written to complain (something he was normally too placid to think of doing). He had received a fulsome apology, and a money-off voucher.

That would be small consolation, though. What Julia really wanted, really *needed*, was something to take her mind off her situation. She had a pretty good idea what it was, she just had to find the courage to go out and get it.

Even so, the phone call was difficult to make. Three times she began to dial, and changed her mind. The fourth time, there was no reply.

The fifth time was a couple of hours later. Julia had worked herself into a state by now. Convinced that Jenny would answer, she tried to think up an excuse for ringing. She could hardly put the phone down and risk Jenny ringing that special number and calling back to see what she wanted. She would say that she wanted to ask Owen something about the college term. That was probably safe enough. What date was half-term?—that sounded a reasonable question. But perhaps Jenny herself would know the answer, and she would have no reason to ask to speak to Owen.

She could see that she might have to wait for him to make contact with her. She dialled anyway. It was hardly likely that he would be in at this hour. After six or seven rings, she was preparing to hang up, when she heard Owen's Welsh voice.

"Six-five-three-seven-five-o," he said quickly. "Hello?" he prompted, while she was taking a deep breath.

"Owen? This is Julia."

"Oh, hiya, Julia! Are you okay?" He sounded pleased, yet anxious.

"Yes, thanks. I wanted to speak to you."

"Fire away."

"Sorry, no. I mean, I want to speak to you in person. I need some help… advice… no, help. I can't really explain over the phone. It's sort of private. Is there any chance you could call round some time?"

"I'll come round now if you like, I'm not doing anything."

There was a pause.

"Jenny's not here anyway," he added.

"I don't want to put you to any trouble."

"No trouble." She could hear the anxiety increasing in his voice. "You *are* okay, aren't you?"

"Yes, I'm fine." She was afraid to say any more.

"Hold on then, I'll be there in about ten minutes."

"Are you sure you don't mind?"

"No problem. See you in a minute."

She was used to him saying "in a minute" when he meant anything from ten seconds to a week. It must be a Welsh thing.

The eleven and a half minutes he actually took were among the longest she had experienced. She knew that he was rushing. It only occurred to her after she put the phone down that he might think she had taken another overdose. As she replaced the receiver, she noticed that her hands were trembling. And no wonder.

She pictured Owen getting into his car, driving to the end of the road, waiting for a gap in the traffic so that he could turn right, and so on, until she felt sure he must be at the door. She looked at the clock, and found that only five minutes had elapsed. He couldn't possibly get here for another five. She went into the kitchen, filled the kettle and switched it on. He would want a cup of coffee when he arrived.

By the time he did turn up, she had taken time to reflect. He came bustling in, a look of relief on his face when he saw that she was apparently in the best of health, with some excuse about the traffic—though, in actual fact, he would have been hard pressed to make the journey more quickly. Julia said nothing very much until she had made the coffee and put it down on the kitchen table in front of them.

"So," he said, taking a sip. "What's it all about, then?"

Julia took a long pause before speaking.

"I feel stupid, now that you're here. I don't think I can say what I was going to."

Of course, it was ridiculous. She should always have known that the words would not be forthcoming when she was actually face to face with him.

He smiled reassuringly, thinking probably that it was nothing much, that she simply wanted him to put up a couple of shelves or unblock the sink.

"Go on," he said. "It's okay. You can ask me anything." The emphasis on the word "anything" was disconcerting, almost as if he knew what it would be. Then, apparently on a whim, he reached across the table and took her hand, lightly. The action shocked her. Rigid, she looked up to see that he was still smiling.

"You don't understand," she said. "You wouldn't understand."

"Try me."

His face was an open book, almost asking to be shocked. He was so innocent in his desperation to please her, to be of assistance to her, to do a good deed.

She shook her head. "No. Please, forget it. I can't, now. I'm sorry to have dragged you over here for nothing."

A look of concern came over his pale features.

"Don't be daft, Julia. I'm your friend. I'm touched that you called me when you needed help. I'll always be there for you, you know that. I hope you do, anyway. The fact is…"

Now it was he who hesitated.

"Look, Julia, I'm fond of you. I admit it."

Again he had taken her by surprise, because she knew that he meant more than the mere words contained.

"Whatever it is, you needn't be afraid to ask."

"What I'm afraid of, Owen, is losing your friendship."

"No danger of that. There's nothing you can do to turn me away, as the song says."

She wondered what song he was talking about. On the verge of asking, she decided that it didn't matter. She rose from the table and walked over to the window. There were birds on the washing line.

"All right," she said, with a heavy sigh. "I'll tell you what. I'll stand here, with my back to you, and I'll say what I'm thinking. When I've finished, you can pretend you didn't hear any of it, if you like. Okay?"

There was no answer from Owen. She turned around and looked

at him. He sat with a bemused expression. After a few moments, he nodded, still perplexed but resigned.

"Okay, Julia."

Later, she couldn't remember exactly what words she had used. She seemed to have been talking for a long time, spilling out feelings and desires and longings. Because Owen offered no comment, and she dared not look at him, she went on longer than was necessary. Then she fell into silence.

It was a few minutes before she could turn around again and face him. His expression was different now. He didn't look as shocked as she had expected. Rather, his face carried comprehension and acceptance.

"Wow," he said, quietly.

"I suppose you think I'm mad," she said.

He shook his head and made a sound that was a little like a laugh. His finger traced a meaningless pattern on the table's wooden surface.

"No, no, of course you're not. And I'm quite flattered, actually, that you chose me to say this to."

He looked her straight in the eyes.

"I can't do it, of course. I wish I could."

She wasn't surprised, but all the same it was a shock, and she could no longer hold back the strong need to cry that she had so far managed to suppress while she was talking. She had been determined not to resort to emotional blackmail, and now, here she was, crying because she couldn't get her own way. Owen got up and came around the table to her.

"Oh, don't. I'm sorry."

He took her in his arms and stroked her hair.

"Don't take it so hard, please," he said. She could say nothing for tears, and she held on tight to the fibres of his V-neck sweater, soaking it as she struggled to regain composure.

"You can't imagine," she said at last, when she had breath to speak. "I knew it was wrong to ask, and I knew you'd refuse, but I still feel wretched."

He wasn't saying anything now.

"Could you please try and forget everything I said?" she pleaded. "I really don't want to lose your friendship. I'd hate to think I'd frightened you and that you'd never speak to me again."

She pulled away from him.

"There. I'm better now. I'll be all right. Do you want another cup of coffee?"

"I think I could do with a glass of brandy, actually."

She looked at him and laughed, as he had intended.

"Attagirl. We need to be able to talk about it as plainly as we can."

"No, don't let's talk about it ever again. Pretend I never said it."

He was sitting down again, pushing his almost-empty mug across the table for a refill.

"I want to talk about it, Julia."

"There's nothing to say," she protested. "You don't want to do it."

"I do *want* to do it. I just can't."

"Let's not quibble about words. I understand why you can't, and I would just like to forget about it now, and not discuss it." She turned back to the coffee-pot.

"Some other time, then," he said, when it had become obvious that she was not going to allow the conversation to be prolonged. "How's your mum and dad?"

He didn't know them. He had never met them.

After he had gone, she wondered whether she would ever be able to look him in the face again. Or he her. His embarrassment was something she hadn't really considered until she witnessed it at first hand, and only then had she realised the burden she was putting on him, simply by confiding in him.

Would he go home and tell Jenny? She thought not. If he did, they would laugh about it together, or feel sorry for her. "Poor old Julia, I can understand how she feels." "Fancy picking on you though!" Jenny would probably be angry. She, Julia, would have been angry if someone had made a proposition like that to Keith. Jenny was different, though. She would feel secure in her knowledge of Owen's character and his love for her. He wasn't the kind of man who played around. Julia sensed that, and it was the main reason she wanted him.

CHAPTER ELEVEN

The next week's class came and went. As the time passed, Julia's remorse over her advances to Owen increased to fever-point, then waned again as she failed to see him and heard nothing from him. It wasn't that she had really expected to. What was there to say, after all? At least the silence proved, or suggested, that he had kept her secret as he had promised, otherwise Jenny would surely have been round to bawl her out. If he *had* told Jenny, though, she would probably just have instructed him to stay away from Julia in future. Naturally, he would have obeyed.

It was hard not to dwell on the implications of what she had done. She re-lived the conversation with Owen in her mind, over and over ad nauseam, until she was no longer certain what had been said or done. She was tempted not to go to college on the following Tuesday, but if she didn't turn up, and Owen was looking out for her, he would feel obliged to come and see her, or at least phone, to check that she was all right. It would be better to put a bright face on it, so as to let him see (or rather believe) that she wasn't suffering as a result of his rejection.

After class, Mike offered her a lift again. Was it her imagination that the offer seemed slightly less enthusiastic than before? She refused, for no particular reason other than that she wanted to be on her own.

As she passed the window of the terminal room where she had seen Owen before, she glanced in idly. The room was dark.

She left the building and crossed the carpark, saying goodnight to Mike and Garfield, who walked off together in the other direction, having reassured themselves that she was going to take the bus—which she had no intention of doing. She hated buses almost more than she hated cars.

"Julia!" She didn't immediately recognise the urgent voice as Owen's, and was startled to see him emerge from the building, almost running to catch up with her.

"Let me give you a lift home," he panted. "I've been looking out for you. I want to talk to you."

"I can't imagine why," she said. "I didn't think you'd ever want to talk to me again."

"Well, I do." He took her elbow unostentatiously. "Come on. The car's in the carpark, for once."

She was torn between a reluctance to get into the car at his bidding and an extreme curiosity to know why he had waited for her. Perhaps he had something to suggest. Perhaps—horror of horrors—he had some friend who would be willing to service her, or perhaps he was going to suggest artificial insemination. Whatever he suggested, she would know that it came from a genuine desire to help, but she would suspect that it also meant he wanted to wash his hands of her.

He didn't explain himself at first. He evidently preferred that they should talk in her house, behind closed doors. He barely spoke until they were at her door, and accepted her offer of a drink with a stiff nod. Julia was forced to begin the conversation herself.

"So what's on your mind?"

It was a long time before he answered.

"I've had second thoughts. About what you asked me. I've decided to do it. That is, if you still want me to. If you haven't found someone else."

Julia could hardly speak. "There's no one else I could even think of asking, especially after your reaction. I couldn't go through all that explanation again. It was humiliating enough…But I don't understand. What's made you change your mind?"

"No one particular thing. I've just been thinking about it a lot. I don't know if I can explain. First of all, I admit, I was a bit shocked by the idea. That I would cheat on Jenny, for a start."

"I wasn't trying to take you away from her, or anything. You must believe that."

He chuckled. "Oh, I know. I'm not that big-headed. I know it's not *me* you want, it's just my sperm." The humour was tinged with bitterness. "All the same, to keep it from Jenny, not to tell her. Even though we're not married, it seemed a pretty shitty thing to do."

Shame was the prevailing emotion Julia felt now. She had chosen Owen specifically because he was a decent man, and his decency was what had stopped him from agreeing to her proposition, as she had expected. The idea that he was now prepared to dabble in behaviour he thought contemptible, just because he felt sorry for her, was not appealing. The thrill of the possibility bubbled up behind her self-disgust.

"Also," he went on, "I wasn't sure—and I'm still not—that it's right to bring a child into the world for reasons like this. If I can't be there to help bring it up, how can I justify fathering it in the first place?"

Julia said nothing.

"Then I started thinking, and I thought of all the parents who do bring up kids on their own, and who do it creditably, and you, a good mother, robbed of her children. You must be suffering something terrible even to make the suggestion. It's such a small thing to ask of me, really, when it comes down to it."

"I don't want you to do it from pity."

He shrugged. "What other reason is there? I'd rather you didn't call it pity—call it sympathy. I could say all sorts of things, and so could you, make up all sorts of excuses for it. But what it comes down to is that you need a baby and it's hardly any effort for me to try to help you get one. I don't even have to own up to what I've done. So I'll do it, on your terms."

He paused.

"Seriously," said Julia after a few moments. "You're sure?"

"Yeah."

She poured two glasses of wine, noticing that her hands shook. That was not uncommon, but it was usually brought about by quite different circumstances.

"I just ask one thing," he said, taking a glass and putting his hand over the top to prevent her filling it to the brim.

She went on pouring into her own glass.

"Let's get it over with, as soon as possible."

She looked up.

"Do you mean, now?"

He nodded.

"Ah. That's not possible. I'm in the middle of a period."

She took a gulp.

"Even if you didn't mind having sex with a bleeding woman, I wouldn't conceive, you see."

She knew, without looking, that she had embarrassed him even worse than before.

Quickly, she stood up and went over to draw the curtains.

"I see," he said at last. "So I'll have to come another time."

She knew he didn't intend the pun.

"If you still want to. Perhaps you need more time to think about it."

"That's the last thing I want."

She let out a sigh. "Look, Owen, ideally you should leave it a couple of weeks. I assume you only want to do it the once."

He looked surprised. "I hadn't thought about that. Do you think it will take more than one go? Is that likely?"

"Well, yes, of course." She knew she had no right to be exasperated. Owen was inexperienced. He and Jenny hadn't tried for children, obviously. "If you don't do it just at the right time, then there's very little chance of conceiving at the first attempt."

He was embarrassed again now. She got his coat from the back of the chair and pushed it at him, propelling him out into the hall.

"Just go home, now," she said. "You haven't given it as much thought as you meant to. I'm not going to push you into it. That was never what I wanted."

"No," he protested, and the decency exploded out of him. "I've said I'll do it, and as far as I'm concerned, that's my decision made. I'll be back in a couple of weeks."

She turned away. "I won't hold my breath." It was cruel.

"Well…" Whatever he had been about to say, he thought better of it. "See you," he said instead, and the front door closed quietly.

Sometimes Julia wondered how Keith could ever have loved her. She had often been unfair to him, and hadn't ever given him the degree of affection he deserved, lavishing it instead on the boys. She wondered, in fact, how anyone could ever have loved her, or whether anyone would ever love her again.

The temptation was palpable. The means were not easily to hand. There were the new anti-depressants, but she doubted that an overdose of those would kill, even combined with the remainder of the bottle of wine. Paracetamol was notoriously ineffective and was more likely to poison you to death a couple of days later than to kill you outright. Violent methods still held no appeal. If she could only have found a cliff to throw herself off on the day of the accident. She would have gone looking for one if she hadn't been so numb.

The wine on its own would have to do for now, as an anaesthetic rather than a means of death. Julia's thoughts crept back, as they did time and again, to that awful day, and the days and nights immediately following, when she had lived in a dream world, not knowing or caring what was going on around her. For the first few days, somewhere inside her mind away from the Julia that others could see, she had been absolutely convinced they would return, all three of them. It was impossible to accept that a thing like this could happen to someone like her. There must be some kind of trickery going on.

Not for several days had she stopped crying, even for a moment. They had to give her pills to make her sleep, strong ones. Now she knew what it meant when they said on the news that someone was "under sedation". She had never expected to be that someone. By the time the effect of the drugs wore off, she was almost incapable of independent thought or action.

That was not the worst of it, either. There was plenty more to come after the initial shock had dissipated. The funeral—funerals—were over before she knew it, arranged jointly by PJ and her parents. Keith's parents travelled straight down from Scotland, but arrived on the scene too late to have much to do with it. As though in a blur, she saw the faces of people she knew, and even some she didn't know. Her mother's cousin, who hadn't been to visit since Julia was a child. People who worked for Keith and PJ in the office. Customers of Keith's. Mr Reeves, her employer at that time, with his long gaunt face, looking no more troubled than usual. Mrs Reeves too. Schoolmates of the boys, and teachers she had never met.

The funeral made it seem more real, but only marginally.

Jeremy's little girlfriend, Amy, aged thirteen, cried more than anyone during the service. Her parents apologised for bringing her, but "she had to get it out of her system". This was said to Julia's parents. Julia herself was not in a fit state to speak to anybody. She had liked Amy, but she had never seen her since the crematorium. Better for the child to forget that she had ever known that family which no longer existed. With the resilience of the young, she would laugh and be happy again, and good luck to her.

It was not knowing that made it so bad. Julia could never know what they had suffered, Keith and the boys, or, indeed, whether they had known anything about it. If she could be sure that they had felt pain, and what kind of pain it was, she could have gone through it with them. Not to be able to suffer with them, that was the hardest thing.

People had been surprised at her reaction to the circumstances of the accident, when they became known, but she was positively grateful that it had been such a freak occurrence, that there was no one for her to blame. The lorry driver could hardly be criticised for slamming on his brakes when he hit the patch of oil. He had been truly scarred by the experience. At the funeral, which he insisted on attending (with his leg in plaster after being cut out of his cab), he had kept trying to talk to Julia. PJ had repeatedly pushed him away.

PJ's voice, as it was on that day, lay in a corner of her mind: "Not now, can't you see she's not well enough? Another time."

"He wants to apologise properly," his wife had explained later, over the phone. "He can't get it out of his mind. We've got children of our own, after all."

Her voice conveyed surprise, almost outrage, when Julia told her not to worry, that her husband hadn't been to blame.

"There's no point in all of us going to pieces," she had remarked, in a terrifying moment of lucidity.

If anything, it had been Keith's fault, driving too close to the vehicle in front—as usual. There had never been any hope of his survival, but at the time Julia got the news, she hadn't been sure about the boys. There was some doubt as to whether they were dead on arrival at the hospital. With unintentional cruelty, they had allowed her to go on hoping until she arrived in person. Jeremy, it seemed, had been killed instantly, or almost instantly. Andrew, sitting in the back of the car, had internal injuries. Not enough to spoil his looks, but enough to kill him within an hour of the accident.

Compensation? Julia had no thought of it, for after all no one had been to blame. Even those responsible for the oil spillage were probably unaware of it. Lucky old them. Yet the cheques kept arriving, compensation, life insurance, accident insurance, PJ's payment for Keith's half of the business. Financially, Julia was better off than she had ever been.

So many times she had worried about them when they were late home, individually or as a group. It had to be this time, the very time she paced impatiently, called Keith names under her breath and eventually started eating Saturday lunch on her own, it had to be this time that something was really wrong.

No one had specifically advised Julia not to see the bodies, but she had found herself gently steered away from the option, by her father and by PJ, who had taken on himself the intolerable burden of identifying them. At the time, she had consented to this with such disquiet as could make itself felt through the mess of other emotions. Later, after the bodies were turned to ashes and she no longer had a choice, the sense of having failed the three of them was greater. Whatever PJ had seen, it had made him almost unable to face her since. His voice on the telephone was always strained and tense, a far cry from the cool, superior man Julia thought she knew.

You couldn't go back, however much you prayed or railed against God; but Julia could have done without the additional guilt.

And it could have been worse. That was the kind of thing people sometimes said, in a misguided attempt to comfort others who had lost someone or undergone some personal suffering: "It could have been worse." She remembered thinking it when a friend of hers had lost a baby four months into her pregnancy—it could have been worse, if she had gone full-term and then lost the baby, if the baby had been born normally and died later, if it had grown into a child and then died. Julia hadn't said so to her friend, but she had thought these things.

No one had said it to Julia either, mainly because most people couldn't imagine anything worse that what she had gone through, but of course there were worse things. Supposing they had died in some slower, more painful way. Supposing an axe-murderer had claimed the three of them. Supposing the boys had been abducted and tortured by a paedophile. Supposing they hadn't died at all, but had been left vegetables by the accident. There was always something worse that could be imagined, and it made not the slightest bit of difference one way or the other. Sometimes Julia dared to feel that she might one day recover from her loss, and other times she knew that she never would.

Tonight she would sleep fitfully, thinking over the things Owen had said and knowing that she had made a bad choice in him. He was too, too good. Worse still, she was fond of him. She should have gone for someone she felt nothing for, then it would have been easy to hurt him. Those she loved most had only come to harm.

CHAPTER TWELVE

Later in the week, Linda called. Julia hadn't seen her for a long time, and wasn't overjoyed to see her now, but she could hardly argue that it was inconvenient. She had been looking over her Russian books, without real interest. Steve Desborough had lent her a tape, to practise her accent. The effort of listening to it hardly seemed worth while. She put it on the machine and lay on the settee with her eyes closed, half-listening and thinking about other things, until the doorbell rang.

It was some minutes before she noticed that Linda was not her usual cool self. There was an air of agitation about her. Accepting coffee, she perched on the edge of a kitchen stool, clearly not at ease.

"Is there anything wrong?" Julia asked, when she was sure Linda was not going to broach the subject herself.

"Yes," said Linda, and continued to sip her coffee for about half a minute before coming out with any further explanation.

"It's PJ," she continued at last. "I think he's seeing somebody. I wondered if *you* knew anything about it."

Julia was puzzled. "He'd hardly confide in me, Linda. I hardly ever see him. The last time I spoke to him was—let me see—about a month ago, probably."

"Are you sure?"

It was only when she looked Linda straight in the face that she realised what was being suggested. Even then, she thought it must be in her imagination.

"He phoned me a couple of weeks ago, to ask how I was. That's all. I told you, I hardly ever see him."

"I wish I could believe that."

Linda's tone appalled her.

"Linda, you don't mean—you don't seriously think—that *I*…?"

"He's always been partial to you. And you're available now."

A wave of nausea sprang up in Julia's throat. Forcing it down, she resisted the urge to grab Linda by the neck and give her a good shaking before throwing her out.

"I can't believe I'm hearing this! Linda, I'm not interested in your husband. For God's sake, I've just lost one. The last thing I want is another one."

Linda began to cry. Julia had never seen her cry before, had not even thought she was capable of it. Insensitive as she might be to Julia's feelings, she did apparently have some emotions of her own, even if self-pity was most prominent among them.

Look who's talking, Julia thought.

Getting up from her stool, she walked around the table to where Linda still sat, sobbing, in a most uncomfortable posture.

"Linda, I'm sorry. I promise you, I really don't know anything about PJ's private life. Are you quite sure he's—you know?" She had been going to say "having an affair", but that didn't sound quite right. Perhaps it hadn't gone that far, if in fact it was not something Linda had dreamed up out of thin air. A nagging feeling that Linda was right persisted. It went back to things Keith had said in the past about PJ being "a ladies' man".

"He's always been this way," said Linda, her eyes now dry and bloodshot. "I've never been able to keep tabs on him. But lately he's been so distant."

"Are you sure it's a woman? I mean, I know he was very cut up about Keith. They were friends for a long time, you know. He felt it nearly as much…" Words began to fail her. She knew that if she started to talk about Keith, she would start to cry herself. Already the tears were there, waiting, ready to fall, at the backs of her eyes.

Not noticing Julia's distress, Linda went on with her complaint.

"He can't help himself, you see. It's all part of the image. Travelling, entertaining, hotels, women, you know. Only I'm afraid one of these days it'll be for good. He'll leave me for someone else."

Julia listened, pitying in spite of herself.

"I used to envy you," Linda went on. "You and Keith seemed to have something. I suppose having children helps. Helped, I mean. I've never been any good with ours. They don't love me, any more than he does."

Gloriously oblivious to the pain she was causing, she retreated into silence, and sipped at her coffee again.

Without speaking, her eyes filling with tears, Julia stood up straight and went into the living room. Barely able to see, she got out the sherry from the sideboard, and two large glasses.

"Get this down you," she said, slapping a full glass down in front of Linda and pouring an equally generous measure for herself.

"Oh, I couldn't," Linda protested. "I've got to drive home."

"It'll have worn off by then," said Julia confidently, although in truth she didn't really care if Linda lost her licence.

What was bothering her, she realised, was not that Linda would think her capable of stealing another woman's husband, but the fact that she was already on course to do exactly what Linda had been accusing her of. Indignation at Linda's suggestion was inappropriate, because she would be completely capable of adultery, if it served her ends.

"I'm glad it wasn't you," said Linda, rather drunkenly, after a while. "I'd hate to lose one of my few friends."

The irony of it all was astounding. As far as Julia was concerned, Linda had never been her friend. It was inconceivable that she should genuinely have regarded her as one. She must have been desperate. She even gave Julia a kiss on her way out.

Torn between sisterly sympathy and a gut feeling that Linda wouldn't have been so effusive in her protestations of friendship if she had had anyone else to go to, Julia pondered the subject unwillingly for a while. If PJ was having an affair, could anyone blame him, married to that pathetic creature with all her inbred hang-ups? On the other hand, he had married her of his own free will, no one had forced him, and if he hadn't divorced her before now it was probably only because he would have had to pay substantial maintenance. Linda had supported PJ through college, and she was entitled to something. But how much? How much money, how much loyalty?

What about Jenny? What was she entitled to from Owen? Fidelity, honesty, things like that, obviously. But Owen had said it himself. What Julia wanted from Owen wasn't taking anything away from Jenny. She wasn't after his love or his long-term companionship, just his sperm.

She rather thought now that she wouldn't call him when the time came.

She wondered idly why she hadn't thought of asking PJ to father her child. Apparently, he had "always been partial" to her, though she hadn't particularly noticed. And evidently, that kind of thing came naturally to him. Perhaps he wouldn't have batted an eyelid at being asked. However, Julia rather doubted that he would have gone along with it. PJ was too clever. He wouldn't want to run the risk of the child support people coming after him with a bill for maintenance. He had two children of his own to keep, and that was enough. The more she thought about it, the more sure she was that the only reason he stayed with Linda was that he didn't want the expense of a divorce.

(What about Keith? If PJ was spending time on entertaining, hotels and women, how sure could Julia be that Keith hadn't been doing the same? It was the one thing that could have made her feel less guilty about the lack of attention she had given him, but at the same time it was the one thing she had never had any cause to accuse him of. To the end he was, as he had always been, faithful as a puppy.)

There was no one else. Mike wouldn't do. Julia knew that as soon as she saw him the following Tuesday. It couldn't be helped. He was unquestionably attractive, but she just couldn't face sleeping with someone she knew so little of. Besides, being unattached, he might want more. He would, she was certain he *would* want more, especially if she got pregnant and he found out. He would be difficult to get away from, once she had aroused his interest.

So she left it, half of her hoping that Owen wouldn't return without prompting, half of her secure in the knowledge that he would do as he had said.

The two weeks came and went, and another three or four days, by which time Julia's better instincts were in control. Owen had clearly changed his mind, and she was glad that she didn't have to speak to him, because to have him come back and offer himself would be a temptation she had no chance of resisting. When she went to college, she didn't see him. It was after the weekend that the call came, and by then it was quite unlooked for.

When the phone rang, Julia was sure that it would be her mother. It came as a genuine surprise to hear his voice at the other end of the telephone line.

"I was wondering if it was convenient yet," was all he said at first. She waited so long before replying that it shocked her when she heard him ask anxiously, "Julia? Are you still there?"

"I didn't think you'd still want to," she said. "Are you quite sure about it?"

"I promised," he said. "I've been thinking about it a lot. I'd like to get it over with now. No offence, you understand. But if I'm going to do it, it needs to be soon."

Julia had meant to say no, to tell him not to bother. The second she heard his voice, her good resolutions went out of the window, as she had known they would.

"As it happens, this is a good time. I suppose you'll want to come in the daytime."

"It would be easier. Would today be any good?"

After agreeing to see him in an hour, Julia's head ached and she longed for a hot bath. There was just enough time for the water to warm up before he arrived. She put on the relaxation tape her mother had given her after she came out of hospital, though she had little faith in its effectiveness. As she lay among the bubbles, trying to relax and feel sensual, she couldn't help wondering if she would be able to bring herself to do it. In spite of the good feeling the warm water gave her skin, there was something inside her body that was working against it.

The doorbell went, ten minutes early. Getting out and towelling herself quickly so that she still felt a little damp and uncomfortable, she wrapped herself in her most all-enveloping dressing gown and went downstairs.

It was Owen, of course, looking nervous. She hadn't even had time to think of how she should behave. At least his arrival had settled the question of whether to get dressed again after the bath.

"I'm sorry I wasn't ready. You're earlier than I expected," she began to say, but he cut her off with a wave of his hand.

"I'm only coming in because I don't want the neighbours to see me," he said, going past her into the hall. "We've got to talk."

"Talk away," she said. "Take as much time as you like." Surely he wasn't going to change his mind at this stage? He stalked into the kitchen and stood facing her, his stance almost confrontational.

"The thing is," said Owen, "I'm not sure I can go through with this."

To her own surprise as well as his, Julia began to laugh quietly. "I knew it," she said, aloud but to herself, "I knew this would happen."

"It's okay, Owen," she said, addressing him properly, "I understand. I knew there was a risk you'd back out. I knew I was asking too much."

"Oh, you don't understand," he protested, his accent coming through more strongly than ever. "It's not the way you think. It's not because I've got any moral objection or anything like that." She noticed, idly, how he stressed the middle syllable of words like "ob*jec*tion." "It's not because of Jenny, even."

"It's okay, Owen," she repeated. "You don't have to explain yourself. You don't owe me anything."

"Course I do. I made you a promise, and I don't want to break it. That's the trouble really. I don't *want* to break it. What I'm afraid of, see, is…well, I might enjoy it."

She gasped. "You might what?"

This was something she could not claim to have foreseen. Guilt, yes. But not fear of enjoyment.

He was blushing.

"What I mean, Julia, is…"

As he struggled to find the words, she reflected that he had rarely called her by her first name. He seemed to be trying to assert himself.

"How can I put it? I'm attracted to you. I *want* to make love to you. I realised as soon as I put the phone down. I couldn't get into the car fast enough. That's worrying, because I'm committed to someone else. I can't kid myself that I'm not being unfaithful to her."

Julia looked away, trying to collect her thoughts.

"If you don't want to do it, Owen, I'm not really concerned with the why and wherefore. I can understand you not wanting to betray Jenny, and that's all you need to say. No. Don't get upset about it, just say no. And leave."

He was pacing around the room, shaking his head violently.

"But if I don't do it, who will you find to do it? Some bloke you pick up in a bar?"

The idea was so ludicrous that Julia laughed out loud. Yet it was something she had considered.

"I'll find someone, Owen, don't worry. Or maybe I won't bother after all. Don't get worked up about it."

"But I promised. I promised, and I meant it. I can't go back on it."

"Of course you can." He was making her angry now, with his protestations and his show of guilt. Trying to find a way out, but wanting to wallow in remorse. As if she didn't have enough problems.

"I'm going upstairs," she said. "When I come down, I expect you to be gone."

She virtually ran up the stairs, into her bedroom, and closed the door behind her. Throwing herself onto the bed, she tried to let out the tears noiselessly whilst simultaneously listening for movement downstairs. There was silence for a while, and she thought that Owen must have left without her hearing him. The front door seemed to be opened, but there was no sound of it slamming shut. She thought she could still hear him in the hall. He hadn't gone yet.

She listened more carefully, then, after a few more moments of silence, she got up, lifted the curtain a fraction, and looked out of the window. His car was still outside, and there was no sign of him in the street.

Then she heard him on the stairs. She remained standing with her back to the door, looking out of the window, and did not turn around when he entered.

"Can I come in?" he said, softly.

"Only if you want to," she replied, still without turning to face him. She could imagine the look on his face; fear mixed with desire mixed with guilt. She had no wish to see it.

"There's just one thing, Owen," she continued as he came closer. "Don't think you're going to lay your guilt trip on me, because I'm not having it. I asked you to do something for me. If you decide to do it, that's your decision, and you're not to reproach me afterwards for asking."

Even to herself, she sounded like a schoolteacher.

"You're right," he said. "I won't."

She turned around as he reached for her, quite tenderly. They moved into a gentle embrace. He smelled good. His chest was warm under her hand. He didn't remind her remotely of Keith.

She put up her hand to his head and touched his hair. Owen responded by kissing her, ferociously, taking her breath away so that it was difficult to respond as she would have liked. She hadn't intended this preliminary exchange of affection. It certainly wasn't necessary in order to conceive—she had thought that he would just get in there and start, probably leaving his clothes on. But even men need some help to become aroused, and of course she was no spring chicken, he couldn't be expected to be ready just by looking at her. She had become painfully thin in the months following the accident, bottoming out at six and a half stone after her suicide attempt, when they threatened her with a milk-based food intended for the elderly. She'd put on a few pounds since, but she knew she still didn't look her best.

She kept reminding herself that Owen didn't *want* to enjoy it. The snag was that Julia did.

She had somehow expected him to be the shy one. She was, after all, older than him by several years (though perhaps, as she reasoned later, this did not necessarily mean that she was more experienced, since Keith was the only man she had ever slept with). Nor had Owen ever seemed confident of his own attractiveness, as Mike and PJ were; no man of the world. Yet he was at ease with his body, and lacking in self-consciousness once the boundary was crossed. The roles were reversed now, as she tried to hide herself from him, while he apparently sought to make this a pleasurable experience for her as well as a duty for him. And he knew what to do to make it so. It didn't take long.

Afterwards, contrary to what she had told Owen, she had no doubt that it had worked. Surely she must be pregnant.

They lay perspiring for some time before he suddenly seemed to recollect where he was. Rising from the pillow, he pushed the bedclothes away and dropped his feet over the edge of the bed, sitting with his back to her. His fair skin was almost flawless. It would probably burn badly in the sun though. There was a tuft of downy hair in the small of his back. She wanted to touch him, to make him turn round.

"Can I use the shower?" he asked, not looking at her.

"Of course. I expect you know where it is. It's easy to work."

He picked up his boxer shorts from the floor and carried them in his hand. They were pale blue.

He was going to wash off her scent, so that it couldn't remind him of his guilt.

There was little to say. Coming out of the shower, he towelled his orangey hair until it stood up in spikes, and dressed quickly, while Julia, in her dressing gown once more for modesty's sake, tried to look the other way. He wouldn't even have a cup of tea. Before he left, they agreed that she would phone to let him know when there was any news. He didn't attempt to kiss her goodbye.

Julia spent a sleepless night. She knew now what she had only suspected before. She was more or less in love with Owen Richards. She didn't want to use the word; it was an old word, a word that had belonged in her vocabulary before she got married and that had converted itself to mean something else when she had the children. She hadn't thought that she could truly feel anything for a man again, and so soon. It was shocking.

It wasn't that being in bed with him had been so fantastic. Twenty years ago, she could have been blind to a man's failings in that department as in any other, but not now. It wasn't about lust, it was about love. Julia shuddered to think what she had done. To seduce—in the truest sense of the word—a man who belonged to another woman, to trap him into making a decision he might regret, which involved potential suffering to a third person as well as to him and to Julia herself. She had always detested lying as the lowest form of human behaviour, and here she was encouraging a man whose honesty was one of his most endearing features to deceive his girlfriend. It was a fearful thing she had done.

In the morning, when she gave in to the light and got up for a glass of orange juice, Julia reflected on her guilt and disowned it temporarily. It was right for a child to be born out of love, even if it was one-sided. The worst thing she could have done would have been to sleep with a stranger.

CHAPTER THIRTEEN

It was only ten days before Julia knew that she had been wrong in thinking she could get pregnant at the first attempt. Her period arrived, a little early, and heavier than ever.

Look on the bright side, she thought. At least it proved she was still capable of having children.

She was horrified to find that there was also a sense of satisfaction, of anticipation, at the prospect of sleeping with Owen for a second time. Doubt flashed across her mind once more. If she called to tell him it had been unsuccessful, would he believe her? She ought not to put him through the dilemma more than once. It would be better to find someone else to have another try with.

Perhaps she ought to wait a few more weeks before making up her mind what to do. Certainly she couldn't phone Owen right now. It had been difficult enough to raise the subject with him in the first place, when she had so little to lose. Now that they knew one another so intimately, now that she found herself so tightly bound to him, it was virtually impossible to make contact and tell him she wanted to try again.

Julia knew what would happen if she saw him again. This time they wouldn't be able to prevent themselves from enjoying sex— or at least *she* wouldn't. Admittedly, she couldn't be sure whether Owen had enjoyed it the first time, but whatever he felt, there would be another dimension to it if they tried again. It wouldn't be a sensible thing to do.

But then, none of this was sensible, none of it made any sense. Julia was doing something quite outrageous, and with an aim that wasn't certain to bring her happiness even if she achieved it, let alone peace of mind.

She thought of Mike. He had rung one day while she was out, and left a message on the answerphone. He was at a loose end, and wondered if she would like to meet for a drink some time in the week. Timidly, she called back, to find him at home. He sounded exceptionally pleased to hear from her. She rather liked Mike's voice, deep, manly, with a laugh she found—sexy. It was always like this when she didn't see him. Thinking about it objectively, she was always sure she could make something of their budding friendship. When she saw him in the flesh, she was inevitably disappointed.

Still not sure that she was making the right move, she arranged to meet him the following night at a local pub. Julia had never liked going into pubs, so there was no pleasure in the occasion itself, it was merely a means to an end. She arrived late, deliberately, so that she wouldn't have to hang around waiting for him. That always looked so bad. At first she didn't spot him, sitting in a corner of the public bar with a pint in front of him, reading a newspaper, not really looking up when she came in. It was a relief when he turned his head and she recognised him. He looked across at her and smiled. He was wearing a green pullover and jeans. He stood up and gestured to her to take the seat opposite.

"What can I get you?" he asked, smiling again, as he passed her on his way to the bar.

It crossed her mind that he might *expect* to come home with her afterwards, that it might be the normal thing for a man like him. He was quite different from Owen, as different as he could possibly have been. She had appraised him carefully from a distance, both physically and in terms of his character, and found him not unpleasing in both respects. That was a far cry from being ready to sleep with him on request, even if by doing so she could get something she desperately wanted.

A major difficulty was that sex wasn't something Julia had ever really enjoyed. When she had Keith, it had been fun at first, but gradually it had settled down into something routinely unsatisfying. Whether Keith felt the same, she had never been totally sure. Being with another man, for the first time, was quite unlike what she had imagined and didn't tie in at all with her memories. Owen had aroused feelings in her that she hadn't thought of discovering again, and new ones that she didn't remember experiencing before. She had thought it would be easier than this to put emotions aside and concentrate on what she needed to do to get what she wanted. That had been a stupid idea. It simply wasn't possible to have sex without it meaning something, not for her and not for Owen either.

Now, sitting across from Mike at a greasy little table, she forced enough cider down her throat to enable her to relax, but it was still not enough to make sleeping with the man opposite seem palatable. Consciously making all the wrong moves, she stumbled through the early part of the evening, wishing only for it to come to an end and dreading what would happen when it did.

They chatted and, very gradually, she began to feel more at ease. Once they had dissected the other members of the Russian class at length, they moved inevitably on to other subjects. Julia still steered clear of anything that would give away her past. If she was going to have any kind of relationship with this man, it would have to be without strings. The last thing she wanted was to make him feel sorry for her. The second last thing was to scare him off without giving them both a chance to get to know one another better. She sensed that Mike was deliberately holding back the questions that he wanted to ask.

As luck would have it, he didn't seem to want to take things too quickly. After the pub, he insisted on seeing her home, and she didn't rebel. It was hard letting him into the house, but when he remarked on the living room décor, she remembered that he had never seen it as it was before, and that made it easier. As far as Mike was concerned, she had no history. Let him invent one for himself if he liked.

He would know, from what she had already said, that she was no longer living with her husband, and unless there was some mutual acquaintance she didn't know about, he must be assuming that she was divorced, though in that case he would wonder why she still wore her wedding ring. She wasn't going to set the record straight, at least not this time. Or perhaps, she thought idly, he didn't care if she still had a husband. Perhaps he didn't mind playing around with a married woman.

Somehow they managed to have a lengthy conversation over coffee without any reference to her family, though Mike did once again throw in a few references to his ex-wife, "the former Mrs Rewley" as he jokingly referred to her. There had been no children from his first marriage, so no complications there. Julia still couldn't work out whether he was referring to his divorce deliberately to try and draw her out and make her talk about her own circumstances, or whether it was just natural for someone who was divorced to talk about their past in an effort to excise the pain. There must have *been* pain. It didn't show in Mike's manner, but it must be there, lurking under the surface, waiting to come out; or perhaps it had all been spent, in the form of tears and arguments and shouting and even physical violence. She could only speculate, because he wasn't going to tell her the full story—at least, not this time.

As he left, for one terrible moment he moved very close and she thought he was going to try and kiss her. Whether he sensed her reluctance and thought better of it, or whether she had imagined it altogether, in the end he didn't try, merely extended a hand in farewell and walked off down the path, smiling as usual.

CHAPTER FOURTEEN

It was next morning before Julia noticed that there were two messages on the answerphone, presumably from the night before, although she couldn't remember when she had last checked the machine.

The first message was in the startlingly gruff voice of one of the decorators she had phoned all those weeks ago. He was sorry he had taken so long to get back to her, he said, but if she was still looking for someone, perhaps she could get in touch with him again. He could forget that.

She had left the answerphone on in case her parents called, and expected the second message to be from them, but somehow she knew, a split second before it clicked in, whose voice she was going to hear.

His accent always seemed stronger on the phone, probably because she couldn't see his lips move and tune it out.

"Er…Julia," went the message. "It's…er…Owen. Just checking if…you're all right. I'll call again."

Should she call back? Having spent all those hours agonising over it and come to the conclusion that she shouldn't, it would be wrong to give in so easily. Unhappily, she kept coming back to the fact that her reasons for wanting to sleep with him again were all the wrong ones.

She left it. She didn't like to do that, after the trouble he had gone to, but he would surely be relieved not to hear any more from her. It didn't prevent her from thinking about him, but it effectively released him from his obligation.

Part of her knew that he wouldn't be easily deterred. In for a penny.

She hadn't seen him at college for a couple of weeks, but of course, this time, as she and Mike passed the terminal room after class, he was not only at his desk, but was looking up at the window, clearly waiting for her to pass. She paused and looked in at him. In answer to his unspoken question, she shrugged and walked on.

"Is that your friend?" asked Mike. Julia had forgotten that she had told Mike about Owen, or at least of his existence.

"Mmm." Come on, Mike, she thought, offer me a lift, why don't you?

Perhaps he was about to do just that, but he was forestalled by the sound of the door, behind them, and Owen calling after her. She hadn't thought he would be so open.

"Goodnight, Mike," she said, turning towards the doorway where Owen stood, arms hanging loosely, obviously uncertain what move to make.

"G'night then," Mike replied, sounding surprised at the abrupt dismissal. Julia was glad she couldn't see his face.

Slowly she walked back towards the room. Owen stepped back to usher her in, and motioned to a chair when she didn't immediately sit down. He closed the door quietly, looking out into the corridor first to make sure they wouldn't be disturbed. She found she couldn't meet his gaze.

"I've been expecting to hear from you, Julia. Just to know that everything's all right, like."

"It's not." She looked up. "I'm sorry, I'm not pregnant."

"Oh." It was impossible to tell whether he shared her disappointment. He cleared his throat. "I suppose that means having another go then, does it?"

"I can't ask you."

"Why not?"

"I've gone too far already. Perhaps it's a judgement on me."

"How d'you mean?"

"I mean, perhaps it's not meant to be. Perhaps it's my punishment for taking advantage of you."

He made an irritated noise.

"You don't believe that, do you?" It was a statement rather than a question. "What d'you think it is then, divine retribution? You always said it might take more than one attempt." When she didn't answer, he pursued the argument. "I thought you really wanted this, Julia. Didn't you?"

"I know, I did, but I wasn't thinking it through. I can't ask you to go on with it. I can't keep making you unhappy for my own selfish reasons."

"Where does unhappy come into it?" he snapped.

"Okay then, not unhappy, guilty, burdened, remorseful, whatever word you care to use. I can't go on doing that to you. It's better if I find someone else. Or forget the whole thing. Really."

For a moment she felt sure he was going to shout at her. She looked into his face, her eyes brimming with tears.

"Don't be angry, Owen. I just don't want to cause you any problems."

"Oh, hell!" He sat down at the desk, next to her. Out of sight of anyone who might happen to pass, he slid his hand into hers. "Come on, now. You don't want to stop at the first sign of failure, do you?"

"Anybody would think it was your loss," she said spitefully, as though she believed the blow to his masculine ego was his sole motivation.

He put up his hand to his forehead. "I can't believe you're talking to me like this," he said quietly. "You're like a spoilt kid."

That was him, she suddenly remembered. The old Owen, the one she hadn't liked at first. For some time now, she hadn't seen that side of him. He had been so gentle, pussyfooting around her for fear of opening a wound. Now, for a moment at least, he was back to himself. And Julia realised that she preferred him that way.

She got up from the desk. Her mouth was twisting and trembling so that she couldn't get the words out properly. She hadn't been this bad for a few weeks now.

"I've got to go. I'm sorry."

She was sure he would come after her, but he didn't.

At home, she cried and cried until it was out of her system. Wanting him was the trouble. It was okay to want a child, that was allowed in a bereaved mother, but to want another man, especially someone else's man, that was beyond the pale.

CHAPTER FIFTEEN

It was several days before Julia heard from Owen again, as she knew she must eventually. She hadn't wanted to leave it like that, any more than she felt able to carry it on. She would ring him, she thought at first, to apologise. But she left it and left it and found she had left it too long.

She was going to see him, some time, at college. What would it be like, would they even acknowledge each other?

He telephoned on the day of the next class. Not even bothering to say who it was at the other end of the line, he plunged straight into his argument. He had clearly been saving it all up.

"Now look, don't slam the phone down on me, okay? We ought to talk, at least. I can't believe you want to give up now, but if you do, then I want to know what you're going to do. I don't want to be responsible for you slashing your wrists or whatever, all right?"

She said nothing.

"Julia, are you still there? Are you listening to me?"

She pictured him in one of the run-down, dusty offices at the college, struggling to get everything said before someone came in and overheard.

"Don't worry about me, Owen. I'll be all right."

"Well…" He paused. "Shall I see you tonight? Do you want to talk?"

"No! I think we've got to be clear. I don't want to see you. I know we can't guarantee to avoid each other, but I think we should try. We need to put it behind us, what's happened. Please, will you do that for me?"

"If you're sure that's what you want." He was sceptical. "I need to be sure you won't do anything—you know."

"I won't try to kill myself."

"Promise."

"Cross my heart."

And that was how it ended.

It didn't make her feel any better. That evening, she chatted cheerfully to Mike, hoping to snap herself out of her misery and into what passed for a good mood. It didn't work. When she got home, she cried and cried.

These anti-depressants had been working so well up until recently, preventing her from crying in the way she had been doing. She had even stopped taking them for a while, when she was hoping to get pregnant. That had been a mistake, because she felt worse immediately, and going back on them had still not brought her back to where she had been in September. There was only so much you could achieve with medication. Underneath it all, whatever anyone said or did to help her, she would still be a wreck.

Christmas was coming, and there would be no pregnancy to make it bearable. She didn't want a child with anyone but Owen, that was the truth of the matter. Not Mike's, not anyone's, just Owen's. It had always been a ridiculous whim, this thing about having another baby. Why couldn't she just accept that she had had her children, and they had been taken away from her? Other people managed without a family.

Becky was looking huge already. It was mid-December, and she was down to visit, with Gordon in tow. Christmas Day was reserved for his side of the family, so Becky's parents had to make do with an early "lookalike" occasion. Julia attended, for the sake of the rest of them, but with no thought of anything that could be described as enjoyment. In return for her effort, they tried not to make the occasion too much like Christmases past. Instead of eating at lunchtime, they ate in the evening, and instead of turkey there was venison, something her mother had never cooked and would ordinarily have turned up her nose at. There were no crackers, and no hats.

Gordon tried to introduce them to a game called Scissors, which only worked with large numbers of people. There were not enough of them to make it really interesting. Someone got the Monopoly board out, and they settled down to see who would be first to land on Mayfair. It was good to do things like this. It could help fill Julia's mind for a short time.

Mum didn't join in, of course. She flitted between the living room and kitchen, making suggestions of more food, nuts, chocolate, more drink, sherry, brandy, advocaat.

"Not that horrible yellow stuff," said Dad. Becky and Gordon giggled conspiratorially. They were too polite to say they hated advocaat. Julia recalled when she and Keith could share a joke like that.

To laugh in her presence was still forbidden, and Becky stopped almost immediately, though Gordon continued, shamefacedly, for a moment or two more, having to make a visible effort to curtail his chuckles.

Julia felt guilty, as usual. There was no reason why Gordon, who had hardly known Keith, shouldn't enjoy himself at Christmas. He was going to be a father and lead a normal life. It wasn't right that he should be so constrained by some unspoken rule that called for extreme sensitivity to her own plight. One couldn't go through life worrying about other people's feelings. After all, she wasn't worrying about Linda's, or even Owen's.

The worst of it was that she couldn't say anything to stop them. If she was to come out with something, like "Don't be afraid to enjoy yourselves on my account", it would only remind them and make them feel more guilty about their own happiness.

Keith and Gordon had never had much in common. Gordon was the archetypal schoolteacher, serious (usually) and stoop-shouldered. He was pleasant, but he lacked Keith's zest for life. Keith might have been physically lazy, but when it came to having a good time, he drew on some secret store of energy. He didn't play football, but he was always ready to take the boys to a big match, or any other sporting event—provided that the weather was good and it didn't involve standing. Julia recalled the stilted conversations between the two brothers-in-law on the rare occasions when a family get-together forced them to sit side by side on her mother's sofa.

"How's it going, Gordon?"
"Fine, thanks. And yourself?"
"Not so bad."

Still daunted by the idea of Christmas itself, Julia thought she might take a last-minute holiday. Why not spend Christmas in the sun? There were so many possibilities. She came home from the travel agents with an armful of brochures. Every magazine she opened contained adverts for winter holidays and "Yuletide" or New Year breaks. Everything from Eastbourne to East Timor. She was spoilt for choice—though she had tried to eliminate all those locations she had been in the past in the company of Keith and the boys. Even excluding them, there was a lot to choose from.

Madeira, she thought at first. That had a temperate climate. Any of the Canaries would be all right in that respect—Lanzarote, Tenerife—but Madeira had a select kind of a sound to it. It would be full of middle-aged and retired couples. She could go sightseeing or simply sit in the sun and relax. That was a recipe for disaster. If she went there alone, she would start thinking, and then where would she be?

There was the option of getting a companion to go with her. It didn't matter about the cost; she would pay for both of them out of the insurance money. Someone congenial. It was strange that, in all the years she had been single, the only person she had ever chosen to go on holiday with was Becky. The sisterly bond ensured that they said whatever they thought to one another. If they disagreed about what to do on a given day, there might be compromise, or they might go their own ways and meet up later, but there was never any harboured resentment. They had gone to Torremolinos together, and to Tuscany. And, now she thought about it, to Torquay. They lent each other money, knowing that they would get it back, or if for some reason they didn't get it back, they didn't care. They never stole one another's boyfriends. She couldn't go on holiday with anyone else but Becky, and that was out of the question, so she would have to go alone.

The Channel Islands might be all right. She could just sit around in the hotel. There wouldn't be many children around, because it wasn't much of a place for children—no theme parks. There would be Christmas dinners and entertainment, but quite unlike anything she was used to at home. It would be all forced merriment, and probably everyone else would genuinely enjoy it. On the other hand, perhaps it would be better to try some country, if there was one, that didn't celebrate Christmas at all. She could try to forget it was happening altogether.

Her parents didn't want her to go away. It was the first Christmas without the boys for them too, and they had always had them at Christmas. More importantly, they were afraid of what would happen if she was out of their sight. A frenzied banquet of sex with all the money-grubbing Lotharios who were known to lurk in holiday resorts, waiting to prey on wealthy, unattached, lonely women of a certain age. Or worse, suicide in some isolated location, with no one to find her at the last minute and take her to have her stomach pumped out.

Quite out of the blue, Mr and Mrs Grant, Keith's parents, wrote and asked Julia to come up and spend Christmas with them in Scotland. On a whim, she agreed, writing to confirm rather than telephoning simply because she still wasn't sure she could talk to them without being overcome by emotion.

Her own parents weren't keen. "It'll be so cold up there at this time of year," insisted her mother. "It'll be snowing. You could catch pneumonia."

The protests were muted. Secretly, Mum had already given in and was making revised plans to go up to Becky's on Christmas Eve for the break she and Dad needed. She knew, as Julia herself did, that a change of scene would be the best thing. At least, if Julia were with the Grants, she wouldn't be neglected or allowed to get into any trouble.

The last week of term, after that last Russian class before Christmas, Mike took Julia aside at the end of the lesson. There was obviously something up, because he usually walked out of college with Garfield, or at least in a group with Julia and the others. As she half-guessed, he had got her a Christmas present, and didn't want the rest of the class to see. Earlier in the evening, Christmas cards had been handed around, embarrassing Julia who hadn't thought of giving them to people she knew so slightly. Olive had given her a childish one with baby polar bears on it.

Mike's gift was a set of coasters. He produced it shyly from the briefcase in which he carried his Russian books, saying he hoped she didn't have some already but he hadn't known what to get her. Julia apologised for not having anything to give him in return, but he replied that he hadn't expected anything from her and didn't mind. She found his attentions touching, and at the same time worrying.

There were in fact rather a lot of Christmas cards. Julia had sent one or two, to her closest friends and family, but in general she hadn't felt up to it. There were still people who didn't know about Keith and the boys. To her astonishment, a card came from Nigel, an old college friend of Keith's who had evidently got left out when she had given PJ the address book after the accident and asked him to let people know on her behalf, because his card was addressed to the whole family. She must remember to get in touch with him in the New Year, if she could face it.

Christmas in Scotland. They hadn't been up there for years. When the boys were small, the long journey had been too much hassle, then when they were older, they would complain at being away from their school friends for even a few days. "I'll miss football practice," Andrew would say. Half-a-dozen times they had made the effort, usually in the summer but once in December, having a "pretend" Christmas like the one her parents had just had.

It was not as she remembered. She didn't for a moment consider driving up, but the train journey seemed endless, though in fact the Grants lived right at the bottom of Scotland, almost at the English border. Parts of England were further north than Jedburgh.

Once, some time in the 'eighties, they had driven there from the Lake District, where they had been staying. They had stopped at a castle, Hermitage Castle, a bleak, god-forsaken place, a big square lump of stone in the middle of a field—not so much a field, really, as a barren wilderness. It had been raining, and the grass was slippery underfoot. One of the children—it must have been Jeremy, Andrew wouldn't have been walking—had fallen hard.

There was some rain now, as the train passed through the more northerly parts of England—Manchester, Carlisle—taking her back to that time. Then it turned to light snow, just as her mother had predicted, almost as they crossed the border.

The Grants' house, far from being cold, was a brightly-lit little bungalow on the outskirts of town, which almost seemed to have a visible glow surrounding it. They were good people, and they had faith, which Julia did not, to sustain them. She didn't know how they bore it, but they did. You would almost think them a normal couple.

It had always been a wonder to her that two such people could have produced something like Keith. He didn't share their faith, he didn't even look like them. For a long time, she had been convinced that they had adopted him and simply not told him. Even the photographs of him and his mother in the maternity ward weren't conclusive proof, she felt.

Keith had lost all but the slightest trace of his Scottish accent long ago, when he came down to an English university. He claimed he had wanted to be as far from his parents as possible, otherwise they would have suffocated him with attention. Just like her own mum and dad.

The Grants had their life, which revolved around the Presbyterian church, now more than ever. They had been good grandparents, but had not spoiled the boys excessively, even though they saw them so rarely. Not at all like her own mum and dad.

Christmas in the Grants' house, like everything else, involved a lot of church-going, and it was assumed that Julia would participate actively. This was unexpected. She had thought they understood that she no longer believed, but she had little option but to go along with it. They took pains to introduce her to the minister after the first service she attended. He was a severe-looking man, much as she had anticipated, but she had not foreseen his dry wit, which came out even in their first conversation. He knew what she had suffered, but didn't refer to it. Perhaps that would come later.

Keith had always complained about the church, recalling the long boring hours he had spent listening to sermons he didn't understand, having to wear his best clothes. Unlike many strict Presbyterians, his parents allowed him to play football after the Sunday evening service, but the football season was always ending just as the light evenings were beginning, and vice versa.

Naturally, he rebelled. He had loved his parents, but he hadn't had a happy childhood. Perhaps that was the key to much of his behaviour in later life. Julia would never know. She couldn't affect any reconciliation between Keith and his parents, if one were needed, except by the act of being here with them, making them feel they still had some family.

Keith hadn't believed in anything, not for years, but the Grants probably didn't know that. Once again, Julia recalled the funeral, vaguely, like something that had happened centuries ago. Mr and Mrs Grant had specified certain Bible readings and certain hymns, which were supposed to be Keith's "favourites", but which, she suspected, were their own favourites. Too ill at the time to protest, she was glad now that she had said nothing and that her own parents, helped by PJ, had taken on responsibility for seeing the undertaker and organising the service. If it comforted Keith's parents, what did it matter to anyone else? Keith couldn't be harmed now. Had he been able to look down and see the service, he wouldn't have minded.

(Funny how we couldn't help using the religious metaphor, even when we didn't believe. If there was a heaven, it was all around us and Keith was with us. Perhaps.)

Her own mum and dad had seemed to draw some strength from the Grants. They had scarcely met since Julia and Keith's wedding, but Mum and Mrs Grant clung together like limpets throughout the funeral service, pouring out tears and memories, while the two ex-grandfathers had their arms about one another's shoulders in fellow-feeling. Julia, excluded from this foursome, had held onto PJ. The rough texture of his charcoal-grey suit had imprinted itself on her memory. She could feel it under her fingers still. Linda had been there, too, on the other side of PJ, but Julia couldn't remember her saying anything.

The days spent in Scotland were a little comfort. People said that the Scots didn't make such a fuss over Christmas, that they saved it all for New Year. Julia didn't find it so. The Grants celebrated Christmas as a religious festival. A New Year had no such special meaning for them. Not that Julia would have wished to go out and get sozzled or sing Auld Lang Syne with a bunch of drunken people she didn't know, with accents she couldn't understand. There was nothing to look forward to in the New Year—unless, of course, she found a way to get pregnant, and that seemed out of the question now.

They tried hard to make sure she had a good time, her former in-laws. Touchingly, they had even found her a kind of boyfriend, a big lad called Stuart, round about the forty mark, single and good-humoured. Julia guessed at first meeting that Stuart had been deputed to look after her while she was there, to keep her spirits up, to take her places. It turned out as she had foreseen. Stuart was there constantly, offering to take her out to public houses (Keith's parents hardly drank), folk evenings, football matches even. He wasn't interested in her as a woman, she knew that, nor she in him as a man, but it was supposed to do her good to have someone to go around with, so that she needn't feel like a widow. She could have gone to bed with Stuart and tried once more to get pregnant, but there was something sexless about him. He wasn't homosexual, or at least he didn't give that impression, but he simply wasn't interested in "that side of things," as Julia's mother would have put it.

CHAPTER SIXTEEN

The dreaded New Year came and went, and so did the rest of January. Julia found herself at home again, with little to distract her. She took to phoning Becky regularly, perhaps four or five times a week, just so that she could focus on something other than her own troubles. Becky knew why, and didn't seem to mind, but it wasn't healthy. When the baby was born, she wouldn't want Julia hanging around all the time, offering advice and generally getting in the way.

She had to find something else to occupy herself. Russian classes started up again, and she saw a little of Mike out of class. Everyone else was a bit down after Christmas, whereas Julia was on better form once all the celebrations were out of the way. For her, there had been nothing to look forward to, so there was no let-down afterwards. The class was down to half-a-dozen regulars now—besides herself and Mike, only Garfield, Olive, Gillian and Rowena came every week. It didn't seem to put Steve off though. He was only too anxious to keep the sessions going, and was already talking about carrying on for a second year.

"I think he's being premature, don't you?" said Garfield to Mike during the tea break. "I can't see the whole class wanting to carry on after the summer." He sounded as though the rest of the class numbered in their hundreds and were some inferior species with which he had little in common.

"I could happily give it up now," replied Mike, "if I wasn't determined not to be defeated by a stupid alphabet."

Julia laughed with the others.

"How about you, Julia?" asked Garfield. "Will you be going on with your Russian?"

"I don't know," said Julia, truthfully. She didn't exactly enjoy the classes, but it was difficult to see what she would do with her time if they ended. Study something else, perhaps. Flower arranging or macramé. Have another try for a part-time job in a supermarket. She didn't need the money, but it would give her something to do.

It was getting much harder now, to retain what equilibrium she had developed. She was at a dangerous stage. Even she herself felt it. The friends who had rallied round in the beginning, her parents and her family, all those who had helped her most, were becoming complacent. They believed she was over the worst, and they could lay off. The reality was that she needed them now more than ever.

Mum and Dad were preoccupied with Becky, and rightly so. Julia did not begrudge that attention. The problem was that she needed them too. Not for any practical purpose, just to know that they cared; and in her heart she did know that, but it somehow wasn't enough. Other friends were likewise missed, not because she wanted to see them, but because she wanted to know they cared. She could have rung them. She could have rung PJ, or, at any rate, Linda. She could have phoned anyone she knew, and they would have dropped everything to be there for her—but Julia was too proud for that. They had to think of it for themselves, otherwise it was valueless. Only Becky understood, and she was too far away.

Ironically, the only person Julia could rely on at this time was Edie Mayberry, steadfast Edie, a nuisance and a godsend. Edie's interest in Julia might arise solely from nosiness, but it was there. Little chance of Julia poisoning herself or slashing her wrists with Edie around. Julia didn't thank her for it, but it was easier than taking the decision to remove herself from her family's lives when the consequence might be lasting guilt and unhappiness for them.

In this new year, there was a need for some new thinking. For the first time since the accident, Julia seriously considered going back to full-time work. She had given up her career, such as it was, when the boys were born, but she had found the time at home, changing nappies and taking them for walks in the pushchair, unsatisfying, and had done various jobs since. The childminder she took on was so good that she was able to convince herself that the boys were really better off with her. Vera had moved to Wales when Andrew was five, but by then there had been no real need for her services. Julia's parents usually took the boys after school, and she collected them on her way home from the office.

For a while, she had worked in Keith's office, helping him and PJ. It hadn't worked out very well. Other staff wouldn't say anything in front of her. That wouldn't have mattered so much, if she hadn't found herself rowing with Keith in the office, continuing arguments they had started at home—then coming home in the evening and carrying them on. The last, and best, job she had taken was as a secretary to an accountant. Mr Reeves had been terribly kind when she had departed suddenly without being able to say when, or if, she would be back, and had never pressed her for a decision about returning. The other office assistant had taken over Julia's duties, and shortly afterwards, she heard that he had taken someone on temporarily.

When Julia eventually rang him to say that she didn't think she would ever be able to come back to the office, he was all understanding and patience. He had even said that she should get in touch with him if she ever changed her mind, and now she thought about doing that. No doubt he would try to fit her in somewhere, part-time perhaps. She didn't need the money, and she didn't want to put anyone else's nose out of joint, but really this enforced leisure had started to take its toll on her frame of mind. She no longer believed herself equal to a job. She wasn't fit to do real work. Most important of all, going back to that office would have meant facing people who knew her and had seen her at her worst. Every time they looked at her, they would remember the state they had seen her in at the funeral, and they wouldn't know where to look or what to say. It would take years to wipe out that memory, and she couldn't cope with the knowledge that it was there, in people's minds, when they were in her company. To work anywhere else, after the generosity Mr Reeves had shown her, would be out of the question.

There was PJ, of course. He could probably find her something, but then she would face the same problem, being with people she knew. PJ would go easy on her, and she wouldn't feel she was pulling her weight. Besides, she wasn't sure PJ would understand her need to occupy the time with menial tasks.

Gardening. It wasn't really the right time of year, but there was a dry spell, and Julia felt she could face a couple of hours in the garden each day. It had never been one of her hobbies, nor had Keith taken much of an interest beyond the occasional mowing of the lawn. One of the boys would usually do some weeding or pruning to get a bit of extra pocket money. Jeremy was always good that way, and Andrew made up in enthusiasm for what he lacked in staying power.

They were gone. Every so often she had to remind herself. It would have been so easy to pretend that they were at school, or away on a field trip, and would be back any minute, their bags full of dirty socks and muddy boots, shouting, "What's for tea, Mum?"

Weeding was tiring work, but then that was the whole point. Planting bulbs was something she had never bothered much with. It was so much effort, and usually the slugs or birds destroyed the fruits of her labour in any case. Even if the plants survived, there wouldn't be anyone to see them, except her.

"Gardening," remarked Edie, unnecessarily, peering over the adjoining wall. "That's the ticket. Good to see you taking an interest in something." If she could only know how much her chatter got on Julia's nerves.

But then that's what life is about, Julia reflected. If something can get on your nerves, at least it proves you're alive. She continued to plant the bulbs. She had searched the garden centre for something, anything, that could be planted at this time of year. What was the matter with these people? Didn't they *want* business?

Fortunately, she came across a book that told you what jobs to do in the garden in each month of the year. It was the beginning of February now, the month of her wedding anniversary, and also the first anniversary of the crash. According to the book, it was time to sow seeds under glass, control basal rot, and prepare for spring planting.

Everyone remembered that it was a year to the day that she had lost Keith and the boys. Her mother and father arrived early, pretending that they didn't know what date it was, but knowing that it would be on her mind. They suggested going out—a trip to a country park, a long walk in the bracing winter air. It wasn't raining much. At first, Julia declined, but while she was making the coffee, she had second thoughts. It would help stop them worrying, and it would probably be good for her.

She had known that she wouldn't be able to avoid thinking about it. No amount of take-your-mind-off-it activities, organised by her parents or anyone else, would be successful. It was a landmark in her life, one that would stand forever, or until she died.

Sometimes she wished that she had had them buried. She had always thought it a disgusting practice, and she knew Keith felt the same. "When I go, make sure I'm cremated," he had said, more than once. "I don't want the worms to get me."

They had abided by his wishes. Yet, though Julia hated to admit it, her mother had a point when she suggested that burial would have had some advantages. A grave, with a stone, would have provided a place to visit on birthdays and anniversaries, a focus for her grief. As it was, she had to be content with the peaceful, yet somehow bleak, crematorium garden and its concrete chapel of remembrance. Flowers could be left in impersonal vases, or simply dropped on the grass somewhere in the vicinity where the ashes had been placed. You couldn't know exactly where, unless you took the step of keeping the ashes. Some women kept a dead husband in a jar on the mantelpiece. That wasn't for Julia.

She couldn't have buried the boys. The thought of those young, unfulfilled bodies rotting in the ground would have tormented her forever. Better by far to know that they were gone to ashes, returned finally to their origins. On the way home, she asked to stop at the crematorium, and wandered pointlessly in the garden while her parents stood a little way off. Three of her four grandparents were here somewhere. Two of them had never known the children, so could not suffer the loss, and it was a blessing that Granddad Bill had died five years ago. He had been a sparky old man, cracking jokes until the day before he died. Julia's remaining grandmother was in a rest home in Scarborough, near Auntie Pat, and didn't know that the boys were dead. They hadn't had the heart to tell her. She could never have taken it in. Julia had lost her too, years ago, without even noticing.

After her parents had left her, reluctantly, and headed for home promising to telephone later in the evening (they had to, to make sure she was still alive, not lying in a bath full of blood or unconscious in a drug-induced coma on the living room floor), she gave way to it. She forced herself to open the door of Andrew's bedroom, for the first time in many long months.

He wasn't there. The room was not as bad as Julia had expected, in terms of accumulated dust, though it hadn't been cleaned since goodness knew when. Things still lay about where he had left them, but the sight of the debris was not as poignant as she had feared. It was clear that the owner of these things had been gone for a long time and no longer required them. He wasn't here.

Jeremy's room was tidy, and she had cleaned it not that long ago, adding tears to the elbow-grease with which she dusted and polished. She had put away the few things left on his desk, so that the reminders were not on the surface as those in Andrew's room were. She almost felt she could do something with this room, re-decorate it or something, except that she couldn't bear to wipe out the last vestiges of her son's personality so casually. It would take more thought.

Tears didn't come so easily now, she found. There had been so many phases to this grief. First the hysteria and the disbelief, then the numbness and lack of interest in anything. After that had come the firm intention to do away with herself, when she found energy from some unknown source for that and that alone and dedicated herself to the goal. Then the failure, succeeded by the knowledge that she had to soldier on. Bouts of weeping and anger interspersed with calmness and more numbness. She didn't *want* there to come a time when she could forget them for as much as an hour, but the longer she went on, the more inevitable it was that such a time would come.

For the moment, looking around the boys' rooms, there was crying and a feeling of helplessness, but underlying that was a desire to turn the tables, to repair the things in her life that hadn't gone according to plan. If she could only have been pregnant again.

Suicide no longer appealed, despite the knowledge that there would be no more children. Julia had entered a phase of carelessness, which in her more lucid moments she hated even more than the anger and hysteria and crying. She had no interest in living, but she had no strong desire to die. Life just went on.

CHAPTER SEVENTEEN

It was Julia's birthday. Forty-two. People jokingly referred to it as the age when you knew "the meaning of life, the universe and everything". For Julia, it was the age at which she knew she wouldn't ever conceive again, any more than she would have her boys back. The most she could hope for was a second marriage as happy as the first, and that seemed beyond imagining at the moment. She didn't even want it.

She remembered virtually nothing about last year's birthday, which had passed in a drugged haze, allowing her to do no more than register the fact that she had turned forty-one. The year before, however, was vivid in her memory. Utterly depressed at the thought of turning forty, she had persuaded Keith to take her and the boys on a winter holiday to try and forget all about it. They had gone skiing, for the first and only time, in Austria. Neither she nor Keith had really enjoyed the skiing part of it, but Andrew had turned out to be quite skilful, and even Jeremy had seemed exhilarated by the activity. On the day of her birthday, Keith had made sure the hotel restaurant provided a cake with sparklers, and their fellow guests had applauded as it was brought out into the darkened room, while Julia herself exclaimed with surprise and feigned pleasure at their thoughtfulness. (There was a video recording of the occasion, hidden away in a cupboard in the spare bedroom until she should feel up to watching it again.)

No celebrations this year, as far as Julia was concerned. Her parents, who didn't quite see it that way, called round first thing. There was a card from them and one from Becky and Gordon too. There were cards from Edie (put through the door the night before), from her godmother (who never forgot her birthday) and from some friends she hadn't seen for a long time. There was a card from Mr and Mrs Reeves, and one from Linda and PJ. "Thinking of you," it said. Perhaps they were, in their way.

Her mother had bought her a magazine rack. It wasn't something she had requested, but Mum said that she had noticed that Julia "needed one". Dad had, unusually for him, gone out and bought an expensive bottle of perfume to supplement the present. Julia pictured him going into the chemist's and asking for the most popular perfume they had. She would never have selected it herself, but she appreciated the thought—it brought her close to tears.

Becky had sent a CD of Rachmaninov, and a bottle of Pimms. Julia could tell that Mum and Dad were sceptical about the wisdom of giving her alcohol as a birthday present, but, from her own point of view, it couldn't have been more welcome. The doctor had warned her against drinking too much, but at the same time had hinted that he understood and sympathised with the urge. Julia pictured herself in the summer, sitting out in the garden with a long drink, feeling lazy and self-indulgent. Perhaps she would hold a barbecue for family and friends, to show them what a good recovery she was making, and serve iced concoctions with mint leaves on top to go with the perfectly-cooked kebabs. Dream on, she thought, as she snapped back into reality.

Mum and Dad wanted to take her out to lunch, and, rather than cause them disappointment, she agreed. It was something the three of them had used to do occasionally, when she wasn't working, so it brought back no particular memories of the rest of the family. They went to a popular chain restaurant, which her mother and father loved and which she herself had always hated. She hadn't eaten that kind of meal since losing the boys. Somehow eating seemed a supreme example of the pointlessness of life. Julia especially couldn't stomach meat in any quantity, and chose a pasta dish from the vegetarian menu. Rejecting the chocolate desserts she would once have found irresistible, she allowed herself to be persuaded into taking a scoop of vanilla ice cream. It tasted utterly synthetic. After the restaurant, they drove to the coast and went for a long walk along the seafront.

One of Julia's closest friends at college had got a job at Aberystwyth and used to write to her in years gone by about how he loved going for walks on the promenade when he was in a bad mood. "It blows the stinks out of me," he used to say. He had died of leukaemia, at the age of twenty-four. Walking along the beach now, she thought of him and wondered why he hadn't told her, even when he knew he was dying. She had thought that particular vein of feeling had been fully mined, but, thinking of Vince now, more tears came to her eyes.

The promise of heavy rain drew them away from the beach and back to the house. Julia's parents weren't leaving her alone until the last possible moment. They had brought a cake, a chocolate one. Even that couldn't awaken Julia's taste for food any more, but she made a fuss of it for their sakes. She cut a few sandwiches, though none of them were hungry, and made tea, which they drank in front of the TV. It was eight o'clock before she persuaded them that it was safe to leave her alone. She looked forward to a warm bath and an early night. Then the doorbell rang. Reluctantly, she went to answer it.

He was, quite literally, the last person she had expected to see. A couple of months ago, perhaps, just after it had happened, she wouldn't have been entirely surprised. By now, he was becoming a distant figure, to be thought about sometimes, dreamed of sometimes, remembered with longing even, but his renewed presence in her life not expected, nor even hoped for.

It had turned into a wet night, and the rain, dripping off his bare head, somehow had the effect of making him look much younger.

Speechless for the first few moments, she ushered him into the hallway and hurriedly closed the door.

"What the hell are you doing here?" she exploded.

Owen stood, almost cowering, his head lowered so that she could not see his face, and Julia regretted the outburst. It occurred to her that he might have come to wish her a happy birthday, but he said nothing. Did he even know the date?

"What are you doing here, Owen?" she asked, more gently. "I thought we agreed that…you know."

"I came to see how you were," he muttered, in a voice she hardly recognised. Had his accent always been so strong?

"I'm sorry," he added. "If you want me to go, I will."

"No, *I'm* sorry," she responded, leading him into the living room. "It's not that I'm not pleased to see you. I mean, in a way. Now that you're here, you may as well sit down and have a cup of tea. Or would you prefer a drink?"

He looked suddenly eager. "Yes, if you don't mind, I would like a drink." He was about to sit down in the chair she had indicated, but, recollecting that his coat was wet, he hesitated.

"Oh, take it off!" she commanded. "Hang it over the radiator or something."

He did so with a grateful look, and sat down gingerly in the armchair.

"There isn't much," she said doubtfully, opening the sideboard. "There's sherry, but I don't suppose you like that. There's some scotch, but it's been here for ages. I suppose it'll be all right." She opened the bottle and sniffed at it. Selfishly, she didn't want to offer him the Pimms, and besides, she had nothing to go with it.

Owen nodded. "That's okay," he said quietly. "I'm sure it'll be fine. Are you going to have one?"

For a second she was about to pour one. Then she reflected. He mustn't be encouraged.

"I can't drink alcohol, Owen," she said coolly. "I'm pregnant."

A patchy red flush came across his pale cheeks.

"Oh God, I'm sorry."

She saw that his hands were trembling slightly as he took the glass from her hand. He took a sip and put it down almost immediately. She poured herself a tonic water. It wasn't chilled, but it was better than being unsociable.

"It's okay. I'm just so surprised to see you. Where does Jenny think you are?"

He looked at his feet.

"She's not expecting to see me for a couple of hours. She thinks I'm still in Aberdare." For the first time, he looked Julia in the face. His voice became almost inaudible, but she watched the movement of his lips. "My mother died last night," he said.

For a moment she was speechless. She knew virtually nothing about Owen's family, except that he had one. She had no idea whether he had been close to his mother.

"How old was she?" she asked, pointlessly.

"Sixty-three," he replied. "That's not really all that old, is it?"

"No."

Other questions were spilling out of her brain, but did not get as far as her lips. It would be best to wait until he felt able to tell her spontaneously.

Why was he with Julia, not with Jenny?

"She had cancer," he continued, not meeting her eyes. "She'd only known for a few weeks. They said they thought they could treat it, but I think they were just trying to buck her up a bit, you know. I think it was already too late." He paused, and looked at Julia. "What do you think?"

Looking at the carpet, she said, "I don't know, Owen. I didn't know your mother, or your doctor."

It sounded harsher than she had intended. Something wrenched at her insides, and she held out her arms to him, relenting. He came into them, dropping his tousled red head onto her shoulder and rubbing his wet cheeks against her blouse.

"I needed you," he sobbed, his words incoherent amidst the tears. "I'm sorry to come here, but I needed someone, and it was you."

Tears came to her own eyes now. His warmth in her arms brought back memories of the boys and the many times she had comforted them in distress. She lingered on that thought rather than opening up her mind to the alternative feelings that were beginning to stir, that had in fact never stopped stirring.

"Owen, I'm here for you," she said. "But you should be with Jenny now."

He turned his head to face the wall, but remained in her embrace.

"Jenny didn't get on with my mum," he said.

Julia sighed. "I can't help that, Owen. I don't suppose your mother would have approved of me either."

He pulled away from her with a reluctance that she could feel physically.

"Sorry about that," he said, wiping his face with the sleeve of his jacket. "I'm a grown man. I shouldn't be coming to you for comfort."

"Owen, believe me, I do understand. I'm much older than you, and you're bound to see something of your mother in me." It had only occurred to her just as she spoke. "But I'm no substitute."

"Substitute?" he repeated, anger rising in his voice. "Is that what you think this is about? Do you think I've got some kind of mother fixation or something? Is that what you think?"

Julia crossed the room and sat down by the fire. "You're upset, Owen. You've come here because you're upset. That's all right. Let's not get into a row about it."

She was deliberately not looking at him. His desperation, his innocence, were too appealing.

"I'll go now, then, shall I?" he said, and, without waiting for her answer, he turned and went out of the room.

Without a thought, she leapt up and ran into the hall after him, reaching his shoulder just as he placed his hand on the latch. Putting her hand over his, she turned him towards her and pulled at the front of his jacket.

"I'm sorry. Owen, I'm sorry. Don't go in this mood. Stay for a bit and we'll talk."

"No, you were right, I shouldn't have come. I'll go now."

"You can't. You've left your coat in the living room."

"Coat?" He seemed to have forgotten the rain.

"It's drying out. Wait until the rain eases off. Come and sit down and finish your drink."

None of this was right. She shouldn't have been persuading him to stay. She should have been sending him home to Jenny. The trouble was, she wanted him here. She wanted him so much that it hurt.

They sat down again. She took an armchair and motioned him to the sofa.

"Tell me about your mum," she said, clasping her hands in front of her and leaning forward as though ready to listen. "What was she like?"

"Like? I don't know. I suppose she was…loving. Yes, she was loving. And devoted. That's how mothers are supposed to be, isn't it?"

He wasn't even aware of the resonance his words had for Julia. She picked up her drink again.

"She used to talk a lot," he went on. "Talk, talk, talk, my father says. Rabbit, rabbit, you know. Liked the sound of her own voice."

"Will your father be on his own now?"

"Yes. I don't know how he'll cope. I thought of asking him to live with us, but that probably wouldn't be a good idea, would it?"

"No." A vague memory stirred. "Haven't you got a sister?"

"Yes, Eirwen. She's married, got two children. She can't have him living with her, although she'd like to. Not that he's disabled or anything. He's only sixty-five. Only just retired. They were looking forward to the time together."

Irony. Tragedy. Nothing to say that would make it all right.

"I just wish there was something I could say," she said, pointlessly.

"Don't say anything, Julia. You don't need to. I just want to be with someone."

Still staring into her drink, she was vaguely aware that he had edged closer. She knew, with complete certainty, what was about to happen, and she wanted it and yet didn't want it.

"Could you come over here?" he said, his face and voice quite innocent.

"What for?"

"I want to hold someone. You know. Just be close to someone. I won't try anything on. Please, just hold me. Let me feel you close to me."

Recognising the futility of resistance, she got up and went to Owen where he sat, on the sofa. Tentatively, she put her hands on his shoulders and pulled him gently into her embrace. For a moment, he did not respond, but lay motionless against her. Then, gradually, he moved into her warmth, clutching at the sleeves of her blouse, tears still running down his face. Once their arms were around one another, there was no holding back. With scarcely a pause, he began to kiss her, deep, passionate kisses that she gave herself up to. His body was shuddering, his face cold and damp.

They did not make love there and then. At first, Julia was not even sure that he wanted to. The kissing seemed to be enough, it satisfied him for an hour or so, until, suddenly, as though waking from a long sleep, he looked up drowsily at the clock and commented, in a voice hoarse with crying, "It's late. I suppose you want me to go."

She said nothing. To say she didn't want him there would be a lie, but the consequences of saying that she wanted him to stay were not such as she cared to contemplate.

"Do you want me to go?" he repeated. She forced herself up from the sofa and walked across to the table where she had left her drink. She picked it up and tasted it. It was lukewarm and had lost its bubbles, but she took a few mouthfuls anyway.

"Do you want me to go?" he asked again.

"It's up to you," she said, without looking at him. "I don't make your decisions for you. Do what you think is…" She hesitated. She couldn't say, "Do what you think is right." That inevitably meant the same as, "Go home to Jenny."

While she was searching for the word, he stood up.

"Can I use the phone?" he said.

She nodded, and listened as he telephoned Jenny and invented a lie about how tired he was and how he had been forced to stop the car and book into a bed and breakfast and how he was going to go straight to bed now. At least that last part was true. And at least she was spared from listening to a string of endearments. His relationship with Jenny had always struck her as rather casual. Familiarity breeds contempt, was the phrase that came to mind.

Then he came to her, a different Owen now, a man—possessed was too trite a word, but it seemed appropriate. Possessed by grief, she supposed, though its effect on him was not what it had seemed to be an hour earlier. Now he wanted her and was ready to demonstrate his feelings quite clearly and strongly, as he had not quite been on that previous occasion when he was deliberately trying to get her pregnant. Of course, he thought he didn't have to worry about that any more.

In the time before, Julia and Keith had made love silently, with the door locked, in case one of the boys barged in. It followed an incident when Jeremy, aged about four, had wandered into the room, seen them under the duvet, and asked why Mummy was laughing so much. Mortified, they had invented some excuse about "tickling". Keith had fitted the bolt to the bedroom door immediately afterwards. Julia hadn't liked the idea of locking the boys out, but had to agree with Keith when he said they needed their privacy.

Now there was no danger of being disturbed. She realised after the event that she could have made as much noise as she had wanted. Old habits die hard, and in any case she hadn't felt like making any noise—but in the aftermath, she momentarily felt an inappropriate desire to laugh out loud.

Owen seemed easily satisfied. He had gone to sleep immediately, but Julia lay awake, stunned by her compliance in the act. She still felt like a married woman, that was the problem. In her mind, she was having an illicit relationship. Technically, adultery had not been committed, but certainly her conduct, and Owen's also, offended against a long-standing moral code. He would feel this too, the next day.

CHAPTER EIGHTEEN

Morning was all too cruel. Julia woke from one of numerous patches of light sleep, feeling uncomfortable, guilty, and dissatisfied. Owen was fully awake by now, lying there staring at the ceiling, his arm lying awkwardly around her shoulders, as though from duty. He clearly hadn't slept much either, though in truth she hadn't been conscious of him tossing and turning beside her.

"I'll have to go soon," was the first thing he said.

She couldn't bring herself to reproach him. He refused the offer of breakfast, almost unable to look her in the face, and left saying he would try not to trouble her again. He kissed her briefly on the lips, a kiss that was dry and meaningless, and went out to his car. Julia went back inside and watched, from the bedroom window, as he drove away. She wouldn't see him again.

The next few days passed in a kind of dream. Her mind constantly wandered back to the few hours she had spent with Owen. She couldn't believe she had done something so rash. It had been quite different from the first time, she had committed herself without restraint. In short, she had felt as though he belonged to her, but now she began to wonder. Once she had lied to him, and said she was pregnant, he must have thought she was a pushover. Only a few months ago she had been leading him on, then she had gone straight out and found someone else; that was how he must have seen it.

She worried about whether he would tell Jenny. He might feel forced to confess now, after such an incident—she expected nothing less. Then it would all come out, about their earlier encounter as well. He was bound to have to tell Jenny about that in order to make her understand. Then Jenny would be angry and hurt, and would perhaps even come round to the house to confront her with what she had done, accusing her of seducing Owen and stealing him away. Julia would look like the loosest of loose women, having apparently slept with two men in an effort to get pregnant.

Mentally, Julia had already begun to prepare her defence, knowing even as she did it that she was behaving in a paranoid manner. Owen would hardly choose this time to tell Jenny, if he did decide to tell her at all. Even if he did, Jenny might be sympathetic and forgiving. If she were not, if it did come to a confrontation, it might be better to deny everything.

He didn't come back, and she heard nothing from him. All was well, in that respect if not in any other. It took Julia a couple of weeks to stop thinking about what had happened. In fact, she didn't stop thinking about it, but re-played the entire episode from start to finish in her head, until she was tired of imagining other things she could have said or done to make it turn out some other way.

Her body couldn't forget him. It had woken up again, reminding her of what she had felt the first time they went to bed together, reinforcing those memories with a beguiling gentleness. It wasn't in her imagination that he had desired her, at least before the event. Love was such a vicious emotion—bringing him to mind at unseemly moments, when she was making tea for her parents, then, when she had the leisure to think about it properly, convincing her that Owen Richards now believed her cheap and nasty.

By now, it was time for Rebecca's baby to arrive, but in time-honoured fashion, it was nearly two weeks late, and Julia's parents were in a state of constant agitation. Julia herself wasn't much better. The hospital should have induced the birth after all Becky had been through to get pregnant. Suppose something should go wrong for her, even at this stage. It didn't bear thinking about, and Julia tried not to. She went, as usual, to her Russian lessons, without enthusiasm, but putting a brave face on it. Owen was never in the terminal room when she left the building.

Every day she expected to hear something about Becky, and every night she went to bed disappointed. The phone call, when it came, was at the very moment Julia had been expecting Steve Desborough to ring with details of a trip he was organising for the class to attend a special showing of *The Battleship Potemkin*—with English subtitles, of course. It was Mike who was organising it really, and it was only for his sake that she was going, because she couldn't think of anything more depressing to do with her time. She would have to close her eyes in the part where the pram ran away down the steps.

"Julia," said Mum's voice. "It's good news. Rebecca's had a little boy. It was a difficult labour, but everything's all right. She'll be out of hospital by Wednesday."

"Oh," said Julia faintly. Everything seemed far away.

"Isn't it wonderful?" Mum persisted, disappointed by her lack of reaction.

"Yes, of course, fantastic," she replied, bringing herself back to life. She felt weak, even though she was sitting down.

"We're going straight up there, but we don't want to make a nuisance of ourselves. Gordon's parents are going to put us up. Will you come over tomorrow and feed the cat?"

It was obvious that they were deliberately not asking her to come with them, because they feared the sight of a new baby would be too upsetting for her. They trusted that she wouldn't kill herself while the cat was depending on her for its meals.

Less than an hour later, Becky herself was on the phone. Her voice betrayed a mixture of euphoria and extreme fatigue. Mingling with them somewhere was concern for Julia.

In the middle of a detailed description of the delivery, she paused.

"Julia, you're not upset, are you? Please tell me you're not."

"Of course I'm not upset. I'm thrilled. Really."

"Only I wondered why you weren't coming up with Mum and Dad."

Julia sighed. "To be honest, Becky, they didn't ask me. I suppose they're afraid it'll be too much for me or maybe too much for you. You don't want a houseful at a time like this, believe me. I'll be up in a couple of weeks, when you've had time to get used to the idea of motherhood. Don't worry about me, I'm fine." She hoped she sounded sincere.

"Are you sure?"

"Yes," said Julia emphatically. "Listen, I hope they're looking after you properly. Don't let those nurses dictate what you should do. Half of them have never had kids of their own. They've got no idea what you feel. I remember, with Jeremy…" This was not a good time to start talking about the boys, especially if she didn't want to start crying. "Look, just make sure you get decent food. Get Gordon to bring something in for you, if you don't like the hospital stuff. Have plenty of fruit, crisps, chocolate, anything to keep your strength up. Don't worry, you won't put on weight while you're breastfeeding."

"I'm not doing very well at that, so far." Becky's anxiety was almost tangible. "It's really difficult."

"Yeah, it is. Take it easy. It doesn't matter if you can't, anyway. Mum never fed us, and we're all right."

She curtailed the conversation carefully with a "Goodnight, take care" that she fully meant but which didn't come out easily. She had completely forgotten to ask what they were going to call him, the new baby boy, her new nephew. Sleep didn't come easily that night. She turned repeatedly from side to side in an effort to get comfortable. She felt hot, and a little queasy. It wasn't right that she should be upset by such a happy event. She dozed, rather than slept. In her dreams, Becky was handing over the baby to her, saying that she couldn't manage and asking Julia to help her out by bringing it up. She woke, laughing with quiet bitterness to herself, at the thought that her subconscious mind could wish for such an awful thing.

Next morning, still half-asleep, she walked over to her parents' house to feed the cat. Fluffy, it was called. Her mother had bought it when they all left home, "for company", but it was old now, toothless and lazy. Seventeen, if she remembered correctly. Becky had been at university, and Julia had been about to get married.

She hung around the house for a while, made herself a coffee and checked all the window locks. Her mother tended to be careless. At least, that was how Dad put it.

The phone rang almost as soon as she got in through her own front door. Mike, wanting to know if she was coming to the film.

"I haven't heard from Steve. Actually, I don't know if I'll be able to manage it anyway. My sister's just had a baby."

"Really? That's great. Fancy coming out for a drink tonight to celebrate?"

She couldn't think of an excuse that sounded credible, so she accepted, even though the last place she wanted to be was a pub. Had she always been such a killjoy?

Mike called early, before she had had a chance to eat. In response to her protests, he suggested a pizza. She knew that he had done it deliberately. He wanted her. He couldn't know.

They sat together in the pizza parlour, and she wondered at his appetite. How did someone who could consume three-quarters of a large deep-dish cheese feast pizza (with extra pepperoni and mushrooms) stay so lean? Looking at him, though, she could see that there were pronounced muscles under the loose shirt, and the forearms revealed by his rolled-up sleeves confirmed his physical fitness. His build was not dissimilar to Owen's, despite the seven or eight years' difference in age. He's not half bad, she thought, and wondered again why she couldn't feel serious about him.

It had all been knocked out of her. There was no man for her. Owen was impossible, always had been. No one else came remotely close to waking up her interest. "I was an impossible case…" What song was that? Something by Abba?

When they got to her door, Mike made his first serious attempt to kiss her, as she had foreseen he would. She allowed him a peck on the cheek, but pushed him away gently, as though she regarded it as no more than a gesture of friendship. She didn't invite him in. Now was not the time, if there ever was going to be one. Mike looked disappointed, but not deterred. He looked forward to seeing her at the film, he said, as though it were some kind of date. She wondered if he was already referring to her as his girlfriend, when he spoke to other people. After all, she saw him more regularly than any other man.

Mum and Dad arrived home with photographs of Rebecca's baby. Jack. It wasn't a proper name, Mum said, it should have been John. Jack was short for John, everyone knew that. But it was the fashion to give babies short names, so there we were.

"I like the name Jack," said Julia, thoughtfully.

"Do you?" Her mother looked at her curiously. "Oh, good." She waited for a further comment, but Julia was not disposed to say any more. She looked at the photographs one by one, holding them carefully by the edges. Some had clearly been taken in the hospital, others at home.

There was a proliferation of flowers in the background. She remembered the huge row she had had with Keith after Jeremy was born, because she was the only woman in the ward whose husband hadn't brought flowers in. It seemed so trivial now. They had still been getting used to married life. All the same, she was glad for Becky's sake that Gordon had remembered.

Flowers conjured up other images from the past. People had brought them after the accident, and laid them at her front gate. A weird and impotent gesture, from those who wanted to assuage her suffering (which couldn't be done) and latched onto this physical symbol of comfort.

Someone had come later, on PJ's instructions, and removed the flowers. A pile of them lay outside the chapel in the crematorium after the funeral service. Still more were crammed into the hearses. It was the biggest funeral they'd had there in a few years, the attendant had told them.

After looking at the photos of Becky and Jack, Julia no longer felt like the cup of coffee she had made herself. It had a strange metallic back-taste to it. Her parents continued sipping theirs merrily.

As soon as they had left, she went out, to the florist's, and ordered a basket arrangement to be sent to Becky's house. The first lot would be past their best now. On impulse, she added an order of a helium balloon, silver, with a new baby message printed in blue and a large bow. Becky would probably need something to buck her up at this stage.

CHAPTER NINETEEN

It was another three weeks before Julia knew for certain that she was pregnant. The realisation, when it came, did not do so gradually, but dawned suddenly. Looking back on it later, Julia could never understand how she had gone through those weeks without a suspicion, oblivious to the changes in herself. She had been preoccupied, it was true, with feelings of guilt and anxiety, but not in her wildest dreams had she thought that the consequence of her actions could be so drastic. It astonished her to think that something she had wanted so badly had been accomplished without thought or planning, merely by an act of impulse.

At first the only symptom was a missed period. Julia didn't keep conscious track of her periods, which had always been irregular, and had been adversely affected by the shock of the accident. She didn't even notice until it was a week late. Then, one morning, after another sudden bout of nausea, the truth came to her like the gust of a breeze through a just-opened window. It was still too early to have a pregnancy test, and she had to wait another couple of weeks before going to an anonymous chemist with a small jar of urine and hearing the word "positive" with disbelief, but not surprise.

Inevitably, her first thought was of Owen, and again she had that unfathomable feeling that she belonged to him and vice versa, only now she knew what was causing it. It was because of the baby. Yes, that was undoubtedly the explanation. She carried a child he had fathered; therefore he had some kind of right to possess her body whenever he wanted. (What her rights were she did not consider too deeply.) That had never been meant to happen, but there was a kind of logic about it. His likely indifference to her was another matter, of no material significance. She and Owen were one.

Julia planned how to break the news to her parents, but now was not the time. There were too many things that could go wrong, and they had only just got over the anxieties of Jack's birth. Half-heartedly, she made an appointment with the doctor, to check that things were all right. He seemed hardly surprised that she should be pregnant. It was only when he looked over her notes that he seemed to remember her at all. It had been foolish of her to think herself so important that he was bound to know her situation. Newspaper reports and all, he was a busy little man, and he had so many other patients who needed his attention every bit as much as she did.

Recollecting gradually, he began to ask about her personal circumstances. He seemed unconcerned by her age. She had had two previous pregnancies, he said, and there was nothing to suggest that this one wouldn't go well, although obviously she was a lot older than last time.

As if I needed to be reminded, Julia thought.

"We'll do an amniocentesis," he added, "later in the pregnancy. If you wish."

She declined the offer. It was an unnecessary risk.

It would be weeks before she could break the news of her own pregnancy to anyone else. She didn't look forward to seeing Mum and Dad's reaction. Shock, yes, she could expect that. Worry, probably, because they didn't know whose it could be, and she certainly wasn't going to tell them.

It was hard to keep the secret. More than once she was on the verge of telling them, especially when Becky eventually came down with the baby. Just looking at him filled Julia with so many painful recollections. At the same time, there was hope and anticipation. It shouldn't matter now that Becky had a child, not now that she was going to have another baby herself. If only it could have been a girl, instead of a boy. Something that didn't remind her.

"How did you think of the name Jack?" she asked Becky, when they were alone together.

"There's a little boy up the road. I liked the name. Gordon liked it. We couldn't think of anything we liked better. I asked his mother—the little boy, that is—if she minded, and she didn't, so from then on he was Jack."

It was so typical of Becky, to ask someone else if they minded her using the same name for their child. As if a name were not common property.

"Mum wanted you to call him John," said Julia. "But that's a bit old-fashioned now. It's funny, when I was in school, there were about seven Johns in the class, and now you hardly hear it."

"Mmm." Becky was frowning. She seemed to be looking at her stomach, and comparing it with her sister's. For a second, Julia thought she had guessed, though she knew she wasn't showing yet.

"How long do you think it'll be before I get my figure back?" Becky asked. "I'm still awfully flabby."

"If you're anything like me, you'll never go back to the shape you were. I'm sorry to say it, but having a baby does have permanent effects. You can get rid of most of it, of course, but you'll probably keep a *bit* of flab."

She realised suddenly how nonchalant she sounded. Becky was looking at her strangely.

"I shouldn't talk about it, should I? It's upsetting you."

Julia shook her head. To avoid giving herself away, she got up quickly and went into the kitchen.

"Another cup of coffee?" she called, over her shoulder. She continued to make herself cups of tea and coffee which she couldn't drink, just so that visitors wouldn't notice.

"No, thanks. I don't want to be running to the toilet. I find…" Becky's voice trailed off, and Julia knew that she was still making an effort not to talk about the after-effects of pregnancy. It might have been a good time to reveal the truth, but she didn't have the words ready. It would take more thought.

"Anyway, it's good to see *you* putting a bit of weight on at last," said Becky.

After the initial excitement of learning she was pregnant, not to mention the weeks of family activity which followed Jack's safe delivery and homecoming, Julia finally had leisure to start thinking about Owen again. She still kept quiet about her pregnancy, for fear she would seem to be trying to steal Becky's thunder. The question of whether to tell Owen the truth was foremost in her mind now. Would he *want* to know? The deal had always been that they would separate and not see or communicate with one another.

That had been when their relationship was purely platonic, or at least on his side. Things were different now, though. He had believed her to be already pregnant the second time he slept with her, and they were on quite a different footing. He had a responsibility for what he had done. And yet not, for she had misled him. Naturally, he had thought it was safe. Had he known the truth, he would have taken precautions. Or perhaps not. It was odd how, at the time, she hadn't even thought about it. There had been no attempt, or no conscious attempt, on her part to become pregnant as a result of his suddenly imposing himself on her. No, it had been pure desire for him that motivated her. What his motivation had been was unclear.

Much as she tried to disentangle the muddled mess of Owen's rights and feelings, Julia couldn't come up with a logical solution. She thought of writing to a problem page. "Dear Marjorie, I have slept with a man to try and get pregnant, and now I am, only he doesn't know, and anyway he thought I already was." And so on. It didn't bear thinking about.

Actually, it was the only way to think about it. Supposing someone else had come to her with the same problem, and had asked her what to do for the best, what would Julia have advised them? The answer had to be no. Don't tell him. You would damage his relationship with his girlfriend. You already have damaged it, but you don't need to go any further. Don't tell him. He would feel worse. You never wanted a father for your child. You want the baby to yourself. He's done his bit. He needn't be made to feel guilt. Not any more than he already does.

She had never thought she could forget about the boys. She had thought they would always be the first thing in her mind when she woke up in the morning. For a long time, for so unbearably long, she had woken up each day with that mental punch in the stomach, and now she sometimes—only sometimes—thought about other things for as much as five minutes before she remembered. Specifically, she thought about the baby she was having.

It brought more guilt. She didn't want to forget the boys. If there was a God, what did he want from her? Presumably, He didn't want her to kill herself, but at the same time He didn't want her to enjoy life. He wanted her to have faith that they were all in Heaven, Keith and the boys, but He didn't want her to go around living it up. He didn't want her to sleep with someone she wasn't married to (especially if that man was committed to someone else, even though he wasn't married to the person he was committed to) and He presumably didn't want her to conceive a child out of wedlock, but surely He didn't want her to be miserable either.

She thought, not for the first time, of going to see a priest. The vicar had come to see her immediately after the car crash. He knew her, he knew she was a churchgoer, albeit irregular, and he tried, he did genuinely try, to give her strength. He didn't come out with too many platitudes. He told her it was quite natural for her to be angry with God.

"One day," he said, "you'll start to believe in something again."

At the time she had laughed, with all the bitterness her body could summon, and told him to go away. He had done so, but had returned several times in the hope of offering her some comfort. He had stopped coming one day when she threw a bottle of gin at him. Her mother had spent days trying to get the smell out of the carpet and make sure that all the little shards of glass were vacuumed up. In those days, Julia could get away with anything. And got absolutely no comfort from it.

"Please, think nothing of it," she had heard him saying to Mum in the hall. "I've had far worse things done to me." But he didn't call again.

Perhaps she could go and see him now, and apologise. He was a good man, she had always known that. And worst of all, he had been right.

Keith had always said that she couldn't admit when she was wrong.

On the other hand, Julia didn't think a clergyman could possibly approve of what she had done with Owen. It wasn't technically adultery, but it was the nearest thing to it. The fact that she had suffered didn't entitle her to make other people unhappy.

She put off the decision.

Her first visit to ante-natal clinic was less than satisfactory. She had almost forgotten the cattle-market mentality that seemed to infect these places. By far the oldest of the mothers-to-be in the queue outside the nurse's door, she was treated with a certain deference, but it still got her down. Anyone's time was more important than a pregnant woman's, it seemed. She had thought things would have changed after all these years.

By the time she finally reached the doctor's room, Julia had resolved what to do about it.

"I want to go private, please," she said. The doctor looked almost shocked. Not many people chose to have their maternity care other than via the NHS. Was it because they were women, perhaps, and not used to demanding better treatment? Julia had never approved of private medicine, but she knew she couldn't stand any more of this.

After that, it was much easier. She could see a doctor at a time that suited her. It also meant that she didn't have to risk meeting someone she knew in the waiting room. She had already spotted one woman she vaguely recognised from having seen her at some of Andrew's after-school events. Luckily, the woman either didn't remember her, or didn't know who she was, otherwise conversation would have been awkward. You couldn't keep anything secret for long. Her parents mustn't hear it from anyone else.

CHAPTER TWENTY

There were plenty of flowers in the church, to celebrate the coming of a summer Julia had once hoped not to see. Roses, gladioli, carnations. The vicar was pleased to see Julia. She could tell, though he didn't say so, just greeted her in the same way as everyone else. No doubt he was keen not to draw attention to her. Others were whispering. She couldn't hear the words, but guessed at them.

"Julia Grant. Terrible tragedy. Used to be such a lovely little family. The two boys used to come to church. I remember them as little toddlers. The husband too. Nice man. Awful thing. Don't know how she can bear it. Tried suicide, oh yes. Lucky the neighbour found her."

They knew nothing.

Some of them approached her. "Good to see you," said one elderly gentleman, a friend of her Granddad Bill's. "Chin up."

She kept her chin up, though she cried during the prayers, when anyone who could see her must have had their eyes open, breaking the rules, and therefore couldn't tell anyone else what they had seen.

After the service, the vicar shook hands and muttered that he would call and see her. She nodded, a sign of acquiescence to let him know that she wasn't going to throw anything at him this time.

She slept badly again, but that was the norm these days. It was one of the symptoms. Funny that she should have forgotten. She had had most of them in her time—hair loss, bleeding gums, wind, going to the toilet all the time. Why on earth would anyone in their right mind want to get pregnant? Age wasn't making it noticeably worse, so far.

The vicar came to the house on Tuesday. Obviously, he had wanted to come as soon as he could, but he had left it a whole day so as not to seem too eager. Even now that he was here, he was trying to appear casual, as if he hadn't looked forward to this day ever since the bottle-throwing incident.

"I'm glad to see you looking so much…better," he ventured. "I know it must be very hard, but you do look a little *healthier* than when we last met." She knew he had been going to say "happier" but had realised at the last moment that it was the wrong word.

"I am a lot better," she answered, pouring the coffee, "but there's a reason for that, and now you're here, I may as well ask for your support."

The vicar began to look uneasy.

"You see, vicar," she went on. She couldn't remember his surname. How awful of her. Perhaps it would come back to her during the conversation. "I'm expecting another child." As though to reinforce what she was saying, she poured the remainder of the milk into a glass and began to drink it.

His expression was doubtful. Perhaps he thought she was imagining it, a phantom pregnancy or something. She hastened to reassure.

"No, I really am. I'm having a baby. It's only in the early stages yet, but it's definite. I've been to the doctor. But I haven't told my family yet. And frankly, I don't know how to break it to them."

The vicar paused for a long time before speaking. So many unanswered questions that he didn't know which to put first, but Julia wasn't going to help him. After all, it was part of his job, "pastoral care" as they called it.

"May I ask, Mrs Grant, how this came about? What I mean is, is it *natural*?"

She smiled. "Quite natural, vicar. I slept with someone. I wanted to get pregnant. I know it was wrong of me, but it's done now, and it's giving me something to live for."

The vicar sighed. "I would be the last one to reproach you, but there are various questions that occur. Is the father someone you might marry?"

"No." The answer came out so quickly that she had to stop and check her thinking. "No. That's not on the cards, I'm afraid. He's just someone I know."

"Married?"

"No. But, well, spoken for."

"I see. Well…The church has definite doctrines on the subject of marriage and parenthood, but we try to temper them with understanding these days. I can only wish you well."

"Thank you. I don't know what to do about telling my parents, though."

He shook his head. "I'm afraid I can't be much help to you there. If you would like me to speak to them, I will. But actually breaking the news—it would be better if you did that yourself. I know it won't be easy for them to accept. But I'm sure they will share your happiness."

She planned for the next day, when her parents were due to call as usual. When they arrived, she cut short the usual pleasantries, and made them sit down and listen. The words didn't come easily, but they came.

Her parents sat, stunned, looking at one another anxiously. Her father was first to speak.

"Have you seen a doctor yet?"

"Yes. He says everything's fine. Obviously I'm a little old to be having a baby, but he says there's no reason why it shouldn't be all right."

"Well, in that case…" said her father, and fell silent. Now it was her mother's turn.

"Is the father going to stand by you?" she asked.

"Mum, I thought I explained that. The father doesn't come into the equation here, all right? He's just someone I know. He's not going to have any part in the baby's upbringing. I've decided that. Give me credit for some common sense."

She knew what they were both thinking, and they were right.

It was a hasty action, one she had rushed into in an attempt to alleviate her suffering. Now they would worry about the progress of her pregnancy, the possibility of miscarriage and the consequences. If it all went according to plan, they would then start worrying about the child being illegitimate, and how it would be cared for and provided for.

By the time they left, Julia felt she had gone some way towards allaying their fears, but there was a long way to go. They had left her feeling worse instead of better for having it out in the open.

"Why didn't you tell me?" asked Becky's voice, on the telephone.

"I'm sorry. I didn't mean to keep it from you, exactly. I just didn't want anyone to know until it was definite. So many things can go wrong at my age. You know. And then, it seemed only fair to tell Mum and Dad first."

"Of course." Becky sounded distant.

They talked about other things.

Nothing much happened, as the days turned into weeks. The initial panic over, Julia returned to her preparations for parenthood. The scan, at seventeen weeks, was something of an ordeal. The equipment had improved over the years, and the definition of the picture on the screen was incredibly good. The radiographer was expert at her work, and said very little, but all the time it nagged at Julia that Owen should have been there. All the other fathers were there. Owen should have been there.

During her other pregnancies, Julia had never experienced the inner tranquillity that expectant mothers were supposed to have, that serene quality she had observed in Becky when she had seen her lately. This time would, of necessity, be different, and the satisfaction of finding herself pregnant, though it brought additional worries, counterbalanced them with a certain contentment that worked against the depression and anger that had ruled her for the past eighteen months. She felt "useful". Other people looked at her differently, now that her pregnancy was becoming visible—and she had taken pains to make sure it was visible, wearing loose, smock-style dresses. It gave her a status childless women didn't have, something she had unconsciously missed in the period since she ceased to be a mother. People generally became more considerate, offering her seats, moving aside to let her pass, and smiling at her all the time.

Julia knew this baby wouldn't come early. Hers never had been. Knowing it didn't make it easier to endure the months of waiting. Russian classes had ended for the summer. There was an option to continue the course in September, but it would be impossible for her to carry on. It was doubtful whether Steve would find enough people interested in continuing in any case. July, the month after which she was named (inaptly, since she had been born in the depths of winter) was mostly very warm, and she sat out in the garden with a cold drink. A bikini was out of the question by the time she was four months gone, but a cool, loose-fitting cotton dress made her feel dignified as well as comfortable, and she began to enjoy—if that was the word—those sunny afternoons in the shade of the trees at the bottom of the garden. She re-read some of her favourite humorous authors—Trollope, Jane Austen, Barbara Pym—whilst studiously avoiding anything heavy or potentially disturbing. She hadn't opened a novel in the last eighteen months, and had forgotten the pleasure that reading could bring.

Mike rang a couple of times, asking her to go out for a drink. Each time she managed to put him off, but he wasn't easily deterred. She wasn't showing that much yet. She could probably get away with it. In any case, she didn't care what Mike thought. Guiltily, she wondered whether she was using him as a fall-back position, someone she could go back to if it all proved too much. All the more reason not to see him, though. If she wanted to avoid doing that to him, then surely it was better not to give him any encouragement.

Julia was halfway through her pregnancy, twenty weeks gone, when Edie finally got round to asking her outright.

"Don't mind me asking, love, but are you expecting again?" was how she put it, not unkindly. If Julia had expected to hear a lecture on morals, she was disappointed.

"I'd rather as few people as possible knew, Edie, if you don't mind. Under the circumstances, you know."

"Don't worry, you can rely on me. I won't tell anyone."

No, of course not. Apart from the rest of the Mayberry family, the whole of the district WI, and all the neighbours—who would doubtless be instructed not to let on that they knew because "Mrs Grant is very sensitive about it".

Thank God times had changed. Twenty years ago she wouldn't have been able to do this and get away with it. People would have spat at her in the street. Now no one thought anything of it. Funny how things go round in cycles. In past centuries, in rural communities, there had been plenty of this kind of thing going on, and people hadn't cared. Henry VIII, Charles II, they'd had mistresses and illegitimate children by the score. They had been able to give the sons earldoms and find titled husbands for the little girls. The mothers were honoured. An irrelevant comparison. Julia might not be one of the royal family, but her baby would have the best care, the best of everything. It was her last chance.

The conversation ended with Edie promising to knit bootees and a matinee jacket for the baby. She would make them in white, since Julia didn't know the baby's sex yet. (There was a bit of fishing going on there, Julia thought.) White was best, that was Edie's view. Julia thanked her, and said white would be fine.

The most useless things, matinee jackets. The boys had hardly worn the many that had been made for them in their day. They just didn't look right.

She knew that the next time Edie visited, she would start to ask about the baby's father.

CHAPTER TWENTY-ONE

He had a right to know. On the other hand, he had a right *not* to know. Which would be worse?

So many times Julia had her hand on the telephone receiver, ready to call Owen and confess everything. It wasn't because she wanted him with her. On the contrary, she didn't want to wreck his life, and for that sole reason she never phoned him. He wouldn't be able to leave it alone, she was sure of that. Round he would come, with his winning ways, honest and guilty, wanting to help her, and then it would start again and she would have to admit to herself and to him that she had loved him.

She had loved him. "I loved him," Julia always said to herself, not "I love him." She didn't love him now, she had loved him then, when they slept together, but not now. She didn't think of him now, except with fondness. Only by putting it in the past could she cope. He was out of her life. He could come back, at any moment, and make it all happen again, but he wouldn't. If he did, it would be against his better judgement. He didn't want her. He wouldn't want her, even if he knew he was going to be a father. He had just wanted to help.

But this was all the wrong way round. He hadn't got her pregnant by wanting to help, but by wanting to sleep with her. He had made advances to her. Okay, so he was vulnerable at the time, but so was she. So he didn't know that she wasn't already pregnant, but what difference did that make? He had made love to her, not caring one way or the other. He hadn't done it for her, he had done it for him, and therefore he had a duty towards the child he had fathered.

In the end, it was fear that stopped Julia from contacting Owen. The fear began when she found a message on her answerphone one day from Danielle Hunt. She hadn't heard from her since that first visit. Danielle must, despite appearances, have been satisfied that she was all right—or more likely, she had a case load that precluded wasting time on those who weren't immediately at risk. Why should she suddenly ring Julia now, after all this time?

There was one possible explanation. Danielle had found out, somehow, that Julia was pregnant. She had remembered their conversation and had guessed that Julia hadn't acquired the baby by honest means. Perhaps she suspected her of something illegal. Julia puzzled over it. Was there something you could do to get a child that was beyond the law? There was surrogacy, but that worked the other way round. If Danielle knew that Julia was pregnant, then she couldn't suspect her of buying a baby. There were all kinds of illegal experiments you could do, but they didn't usually result in a normal pregnancy.

Then a terrible thought added itself spontaneously to the list of possibilities. Danielle didn't think Julia was fit to be a mother. She wanted to have the baby taken from her, taken into care. Oh God, please no.

Julia thought of ignoring the message. If she did that, though, it might make things worse. Supposing Danielle came round to the house, saw what a state she was in, started some kind of observation on her, started calling regularly? Better to phone back and get it over with.

The first time she tried, she got the answerphone. Unable to think what kind of message she could leave that wouldn't give her away, she hung up, intending to try again later.

How had Danielle found out? The hospital, obviously, or maybe—the vicar? No, surely not. Julia had spoken to him in confidence. Weren't vicars like doctors and solicitors, unable to reveal details of their clients' business to a third party? More likely there was some tie-up between the medical people and the social services, something that would trigger an action on Danielle's part. She left it for a couple of hours before trying again. This time Danielle herself answered the phone.

"Hello," said Julia, hoping her voice didn't betray her anxiety. "It's Julia Grant. You left a message for me."

"Oh, yes, Julia. Just a moment, please." The sound of papers being moved around could be heard. "Yes, Julia, I called on you some time ago, do you remember?"

Of course I bloody remember, Julia wanted to say. How could I forget an idiot like you? No, that was unfair, and even if it had been justified, she couldn't have said it.

"Yes, I remember."

Was it possible that Danielle herself didn't remember?

"I wondered how you were getting on, and if you'd be requiring any more visits."

A bluff. It had to be a bluff.

"I'm fine, thank you. I don't think I need to bother you at present."

"Only I have to keep in touch, you see. Did I explain to you that we keep notes on people we've been in contact with?"

"Yes, you did."

"And you're sure you're all right?"

"Yes, I'm fine."

"In that case, I'll put 'No further action' on your notes. That means we won't contact you unless you get in touch with us. Is that okay?"

Julia gulped.

"You've still got our number, haven't you?" Danielle continued. "Yes, of course, silly question, you couldn't have made this call if you didn't have it, could you?" She laughed reassuringly.

"I've got it, but I don't think I'll need it."

"No. Well, that's great! Goodbye, then, Julia. Don't forget we're always here if you need us."

"I'll remember that. Thanks."

Could it really have been so easy to get them off her back? Was Danielle bluffing, did she know about the baby or not? She had sounded genuinely ignorant of Julia's circumstances. She didn't even sound as if she remembered their conversation.

All the same, it helped Julia make up her mind that it was better not to say anything to Owen, just in case. Once the social services found out about him, they'd come down on him like a ton of bricks, trying to get him to pay maintenance and so forth. Then Jenny would find out, and everything would go pear-shaped. No, better to keep the secret. He didn't need to know.

Activity was the best thing. Activity, constant activity, would help Julia to forget Owen. She knew it wouldn't be wise to start doing a lot in the garden, but perhaps a few longish walks into town and around the park. When the weather became more changeable, she tried to do more around the house. She was putting on weight rapidly now. Everything was tiring, even a bit of vacuuming in the living room, the only room she cleaned most days because it was the only room she really used. The kitchen and bathroom only needed a quick going-over once a week.

"You're trying to do too much," Mum warned when she saw her dusting. "Let me do that for you. You go and sit down."

"I'm all right, Mum, don't worry about me."

Her parents' attitude was over the top, especially Mum. It was natural for them to be concerned, so Julia tried not to snap at them too often, but it was always a relief when they went home. That was the time when she relaxed, sat around and watched television or listened to music. Mendelssohn's Violin Concerto, the second movement, had always made her think of her grandfather. She didn't really know why, but it was a pleasant reminder, not a painful one. It was better than listening to pop music—which never failed to remind her of the boys, or if it was 'seventies' or 'eighties' stuff, of Keith.

Next morning, Julia started to bleed. She was having a miscarriage.

It was inevitable. She didn't deserve to have another child, not after the way she had let the first two go, not after the way she had gone about replacing them. Her mother had warned her, and she had ignored the warning, showing that she couldn't even look after an unborn baby properly. She should never have told anyone that she was pregnant. She should have kept up the pretence until the last possible moment. Now it wouldn't happen, as she had always secretly known it wouldn't.

It happened in the biggest department store in town, where she was looking avariciously at expensive nursery furniture. She felt something, she wasn't sure what, but enough to alarm her and send her running to the toilet—or the Ladies' Powder Room, as they quaintly put it.

The taxi rank was right outside the store. For once, walking would have been out of the question, even to the nearest bus stop. Julia took a cab straight to the hospital. There was no point going to the doctor first. If she was going to have a miscarriage, she might as well do it in a place where she could be cared for and given proper treatment. It would be the third child she had lost. She had never known this one, but it didn't make it any easier.

They put her in bed. People came and went, looking at her, examining her, checking her blood pressure, temperature, age, weight, height, name and address. Ironic that she should begin to be reminded of what it was like to be having a baby. The procedures were almost the same; it was just the outcome that differed. There was surprisingly little pain. They asked who should be contacted, who should be informed that Julia was in hospital.

"Nobody," she answered. "There's nobody."

For her parents, it was just another ordeal that she would rather not put them through.

Julia cried, and then stopped. It wasn't at all like when she had lost the boys. The numbness came straight away. The nurses uttered the usual platitudes, but they had no idea of her feelings. They couldn't know.

A sense of powerlessness inundated her. Thinking you could take control of your life was always a mistake. Just when you thought you had it made, something was sure to happen to spoil everything. This had always been going to happen. She had even foreseen it when she tried to seduce Owen. There had never been the slightest possibility that she could recoup her losses by getting pregnant, no, not the slightest. She had been marked out by destiny for unhappiness, and that was how it was going to be from now on. Unhappiness wasn't a strong enough word. Misery came closer to it. And she must have done something to deserve it.

She hadn't even appreciated how lucky she was to be pregnant. After all that planning, all she could think of was how to tell her parents, how to tell Owen, what people would think of her. She hadn't thought at all about her future, about the baby and how she would bring it up—how she would have brought it up, if it had been born. She had forgotten to thank God. This was probably His way of punishing her. Ha ha, Julia Grant, you thought you could start going to church again whenever you felt like it, didn't you? Well, yah boo, sucks to you!

Julia lay in bed for hours, sometimes weeping quietly at the thought of her misfortunes, sometimes just lying there motionless, without any real feeling. Night fell. As she dozed, she was suddenly overwhelmed by the knowledge that her parents would be looking for her. They would have telephoned, and, having failed to get an answer or a return call within a few hours, they would have gone to the house to look for her. They had the key. Finding her missing, they would call the police.

After a few minutes of panic and soul-searching, she remembered that they were away, visiting Becky again, having left that very morning. Even if they couldn't get an answer, they wouldn't be able to come looking for her. There was no immediate need for hysteria, though she felt a slight uneasiness about the cat, who would be forced to forage for food. Her muscles relaxed, and she felt drowsy, as though she could sleep. Something they had given her, here in the hospital, to lessen the blow of loss?

It was morning. Julia was offered breakfast, a bowl of soggy cornflakes and a piece of soggy toast. She rejected them.

"Come on now, Mrs Grant, we must keep our strength up. Remember you're expecting."

The nurse's words didn't sink in for a while.

Another doctor, an Arab, was doing his rounds. He took Julia's pulse, then brought out the instrument, like an egg-cup, for listening to the baby's heartbeat. Her belly, rising from the bedclothes in front of her, was still mountainous.

"Doctor," she brought herself to say, though her voice sounded like a stranger's, "haven't I had a miscarriage?"

The doctor smiled. "Why no, Mrs…"—he glanced at her notes—"Mrs Grant. You've had some bleeding, but not a miscarriage. Complete bed-rest, that's what you need. Been overdoing it?"

It wasn't really a question, so Julia didn't bother to answer. The inside of her brain was filled with the wonder of it. She *was* still pregnant, she was. There was hope. Another child might still be born.

"Are you sure?" she asked, suspiciously.

"Yes, Mrs Grant. Don't worry. We'll get you through this. The baby's fine. Just a little loss of blood, that's all. It happens sometimes."

"You're sure about this, are you?" she asked, after a moment's thought. "I mean, if you're not sure, please don't say it's all right, because I've been through enough."

He didn't seem to know what she meant. Hospitals weren't that well co-ordinated, even in these days of computer systems and community medicine. Her records were no doubt somewhere else, and there was no indication on the notes at the end of the bed that she was a basket case.

"Yes, Mrs Grant. You mustn't worry, because that only puts you at risk. You're how old? Forty-three?"

"Forty-two," she corrected, indignantly.

"Forty-two, yes. I'm sure you know the risks of pregnancy at your age. But as long as you look after yourself, there's no reason why you shouldn't carry to full term. Take it easy now, don't get excited or upset about anything. This was just a little warning to you not to overdo things."

Julia fell back against the pillows.

No miscarriage after all, then. It looked as though she might actually be allowed to have this baby, wicked as she had been. Nevertheless, she was glad that she hadn't allowed herself the luxury of going shopping for baby things. Her mother had been outraged when she had declared that she would not buy *anything*, not a single thing, until the baby was born and she could hold it in her arms.

"At least get something for him to sleep in," her mother had argued, "and some vests and nappies, you'll need those whatever happens."

Rebecca had come to the rescue, insisting that she had everything Julia could possibly need, left over from when Jack was tiny. He had grown out of his carry-cot already, and all his new-born clothing and underwear. There were bottles, too, and a sterilising unit. It didn't stop people, specifically Mum and Dad, buying presents well in advance of the birth, but at least she didn't have piles of stuff in the house she might never use, if the baby didn't survive. All those sad reminders, as if there weren't enough of them around already.

Not that it hadn't been a temptation. Every time Julia passed a baby shop, or glimpsed a mail-order catalogue, she wanted to buy the lot. Her child, her new and last child, would want for nothing. Recognising the urge as mere self-indulgence, she had refrained, and now she knew it had been the sensible thing.

Later that day, her parents showed up. Edie had called them. She had found out where Julia was by the simple expedient of ringing the hospital.

"Mum, Dad, I thought you were at Becky's."

"Oh, Julia!" Her mother was distraught. "Why didn't you phone, or at least leave a message? Even Edie didn't know where you were."

Even Edie? Did they think Edie was her closest confidante? Did she look that desperate? Now she realised that Edie had been in cahoots with her parents all along, keeping them informed, holding emergency telephone numbers, just in case she did a disappearing act while they were away.

"I didn't think of it, Mum. I'm sorry. It was all so sudden. I came straight to the hospital when the bleeding started."

"But you haven't had a miscarriage. At least, that's what the nurse said. You're all right? The baby's all right?"

Already they were grandparents-to-be again.

Julia cursed herself for putting them through it. She should have had more sense. What was she playing at, trying to have a baby at forty-two, just so as not to be outdone by her little sister?

When they let her out, Mum and Dad insisted on taking her home and "making her comfortable". To their credit, they never referred to their previous warnings about over-activity, but they were insistent that she wasn't to do *anything*. Mum wanted her to lie straight down on the sofa, with a table alongside holding everything she could possibly want. Magazines, books, the remote control for the television, even a kettle. Mum had been here already, rearranging things.

"I thought," she said, with timid enthusiasm, "that it would be easier if you didn't have to get up every time you want a cup of tea. You see, you've got your kettle here, and your coffee and teabags, and I bought this dried milk so that you don't even need to go to the fridge."

"I hate dried milk," said Julia.

"Oh. Well, I don't know what to do then. The whole point is that you get complete rest. You know, the doctor said so."

"I don't think he meant I had to lie down all the time. Besides, exercise is important when you're pregnant. And there are more vitamins in fresh milk."

"Ah, now I don't think that's true. See what it says, here on the label…"

"Eileen," interrupted Julia's father.

Mum broke off and looked at him anxiously, her eyes moist.

"I'm only trying to help."

"Yes, I know, but perhaps Julia needs a bit of space." That sounded strange somehow. It wasn't an expression Dad would normally have used. Julia suspected he had picked it up from Gordon.

"Of course." Mum was offended now. "I didn't mean to interfere. Of course, she must do as she likes, as long as she takes care of herself." She turned away, to cry no doubt. Julia pretended not to notice.

Dad smiled falsely. "We'll come over to see you as often as you like, Julia. Rebecca's going to come down at the weekend. Will it be all right if she brings Jack? She can't leave him, really, but she doesn't want to disturb you."

"I'd love to see Jack." Julia was telling the truth, for once.

CHAPTER TWENTY-TWO

Julia cooed over her little nephew with enthusiasm. She and Becky sat, enjoying the autumn sunshine, in their parents' conservatory. It was so long since they had sat like this together, and now there was a new dimension in their relationship.

Julia watched her sister, noting the changes motherhood had brought. Becky's every movement was smooth and patient. She had always been quieter and more gentle than Julia, but now she was positively Madonna-like, like a statue, almost. Her hair fell forward as she bent over the carry-cot, and Julia thought how much she loved her, probably as much as Gordon did, if not more.

"There are so many different kinds of love," she said.

"Mmm," said Becky, picking up her baby and holding him against her chest. "I never imagined how much it's possible to love a child."

Almost immediately, her face went white.

"I'm sorry. I shouldn't."

Julia shook her head. "It's all right."

"I never realised, till I had Jack, how much you'd lost. I couldn't conceive of that much love. When I started to think about it, I just couldn't bear it."

"I know. Don't think about it, it'll only get you down, and I certainly don't want to dwell on it. Think happy thoughts, as Mum would say."

Becky laughed lightly. "Did she say that to you when you were expecting, too? She told me to play beautiful music."

"And did you?"

"I compromised on Sade. I know that wasn't what she meant, but I found it soothing. And the baby loves the *Diamond Life* album. It never fails to send him to sleep."

It was funny how people started referring to their new child as "the baby," even when it had a perfectly good name. Something to do with roles? The function of the baby was to be babied. The function of the mother was to do the babying. The function of the father—well, that was still a mystery sometimes.

"How's Gordon been?"

"Oh, fine. Though I suspect he'd rather have had a girl."

"Really?" Julia knew the reasons full well, but conversation was necessary.

"He won't be happy about all those football matches and things. He's no good at outdoor activities, and he'll worry that he's not being a proper father."

"Maybe Jack won't be that sort of boy. Maybe he won't be interested in sport."

"Oh no, Gordon will make sure he is. He keeps saying he doesn't want Jack to turn out like him. I think he always felt a bit of an outsider at school."

Nothing was said for a while.

"You and Gordon are very well suited," commented Julia eventually.

"Oh, do you think so?"

It came as a surprise.

"Don't *you* think so?"

"People say so."

"But you are happy, aren't you?"

Becky was silent for a minute, engrossed in checking Jack's nappy for damage.

"Yes, I suppose so."

Julia had thought all marriages were happy except her own.

"There isn't anything wrong, is there?" She couldn't think how else to phrase the question, but she realised, even as she asked it, that she was asking a closed question, inviting a negative response. What she should have asked was "Is there anything wrong?" or even "What's wrong?"

"No, there's nothing wrong exactly. I just sometimes wonder."

"Go on."

"I don't know how to put it. You and Keith, when you were married, did you ever feel that other things were more important?"

"What kind of other things?" Despite all the practice she'd had at the receiving end, Julia didn't feel qualified for this kind of counselling.

"Children, for a start." Becky looked up nervously. "I'm sorry to bring it up again."

"Oh, that. Don't worry about that. It's only natural that you should feel you love Jack more than Gordon. After all, he needs you more."

"If only that were true. But one of the things about Gordon is, he's so clingy."

"Do you mean he's jealous of the baby?"

"No, not just that. He's always been that way. He can't leave me alone, he always has to be with me. You wouldn't believe the trouble I had just getting away for the weekend."

The conversation ended there. Julia didn't want to hear her sister's marital troubles. She loved Becky, but she had to maintain an idealised view of them as a family. It was no good her slipping into the disillusionment that had marred her own marriage. Becky was good and sweet, Gordon was loving and dependable, Jack was—well, a baby—and their parents gave both Julia and Becky the kind of unconditional love that the girls would give to their own children in years to come. It all felt good. There was no scope for it all to break down.

All too soon Becky was gone again, and Julia had no one to share her fears. Becky hadn't asked much about the origins of the pregnancy. Of course, there wouldn't be much point if it came to an abrupt termination, as perhaps they were all anticipating, despite the recent reprieve.

Julia had rung Steve Desborough at the beginning of September to say it wasn't possible for her to continue with her Russian classes. He wasn't very good at pretending to be sorry, although in truth she thought that he probably *was* sorry, because every student he lost made it less likely that the classes would go on. He just wasn't good at sounding genuine. The poor lad had real personality problems.

She hadn't seen Mike face-to-face since the summer. The day he called, Julia wasn't expecting anyone. Heaving herself up from the chair, she went to the door slowly, rubbing her back where it ached from lolling unsupported for too long.

His face, when he saw her, was a picture.

"Julia," he began, smiling as usual, and broke off immediately when he noticed the size of her frontage. His eyes moved down her body, and back up to her face.

"Oh, my God," he said slowly. The smile had disappeared. "I'm sorry. I didn't know you were…"

"Well, as you see, I am. Would you like to come in?"

In a curious way, she found that she was pleased to see him.

"What brings you this way?"

"I was just passing. Honestly, I was. I've missed you since classes started back, so I thought I'd call in. I had no idea that you were, er, expecting."

"I suppose you thought I was too old."

Vigorous head-shaking accompanied his denial, though she noticed he almost fell into the armchair she had indicated to him.

"No! Certainly not. You're only—however old you are. I hadn't thought about your age at all. But you see, I always thought you were…"

"Unattached?"

He blushed, something she had not thought him capable of. "Er, yes. I thought you'd have mentioned it by now if you were with someone."

"With someone." How tactful. People like Mike could always find some euphemism, she reflected.

"Actually, I'm not *with* anyone. I'm not married, engaged or even living with anyone. I just happen to be pregnant."

"Oh." Was it her imagination, or did he look pleased? "And how is it going so far?"

"Bit of a scare the other day. I thought I'd lost it. But it seems it's okay. I've just got to take it easy now, and not overdo it."

Looking around the room, he twiddled his fingers.

"I suppose that puts the kibosh on the idea of taking you out for a drink, then?" he said.

"Not at all. I could do with a break from the usual routine. I wouldn't want to go far, though. I'm not supposed to exert myself."

"Great." Mike leapt up. "There are plenty of options nearby. In any case, I'm driving, so you won't have to walk a step if you don't want to."

Julia knew that it was a kind of devilment that was operating on her. She would never have gone out with Mike with so little hesitation if she had still been innocent. All the world could see her on his arm now, for all she cared, including Edie and any other neighbours who might be interested. In fact, she rather hoped they might be watching from behind their venetian blinds as she walked out to his car.

It was safe. It wouldn't make any difference to Mike that she was unattached. All he could see was the size of her belly, and that gave the clearest possible "hands-off" message. If he was still attracted to her, as he seemed to be, it would be in the most innocent way. At the same time, any stranger seeing her with him would assume they were a married couple, and she didn't mind that either. Rather, she relished it. She had been too long on her own.

Mike didn't ask about the father. She hadn't supposed he would. It was odd how nearly everyone side-stepped the question, even Becky. People were so damn polite. Inside, Julia was aching to tell everyone about Owen, about his beauty, his passion, his irresistibility and about how angry he made her.

It wasn't fair to Mike to make him think she was available, though. She spoke to him in a friendly yet distant manner, making him work hard for any sign of affection from her. After all these months, she was still wondering what kind of father he would have made for her baby. What kind of father he could still make, possibly, if she thought the child needed one?

The baby was moving a lot. It always seemed to happen when she was sitting still, or perhaps it was just that it was more noticeable then. The first time had come as a shock, that unmistakable "butterfly" feeling, which she only half-remembered, yet which she recognised as soon as she felt it. Nowadays the feeling was different, more like having a vehicle carrying out a three-point-turn inside you, with little room for manoeuvre. When the baby turned, and its head engaged, which would be soon, there wouldn't be long to wait for the birth.

"Are you feeling all right?" Mike asked, noticing how she shuffled uncomfortably in the chair.

"I'm fine. The baby's kicking rather a lot, that's all."

"I can see him moving." Funny how everyone referred to unborn babies as "he" and "him". It would have sounded very strange if Mike had said, "I can see her," even though there was a fifty-fifty chance that it was a girl.

They got up to leave the wine bar.

"May I feel the baby?" he asked suddenly, moving his hand hesitantly towards her tummy.

"Of course," she said, unwillingly. He held his hand over the womb for a few moments. It felt warm, and he seemed to experience no unease, as so many men would have done. She looked down, observing the veins on the back of his hand and the coarse brown hair beginning at the wrist. A naturally domesticated man, comfortable in the presence of women and children, exactly the kind of man she needed.

When he dropped her off—the phrase "dropped off" didn't really seem to apply to a woman who weighed in at nearly eleven stone and carried it all up front—he got out and opened the car door, asked her if she wanted him to come in and if she needed anything. Having received a negative reply, he kissed her on the lips, touched her arm and smiled again. Julia felt warm as she entered the house and waved back at the car.

There might be some point in it. Mike was okay. He was attractive in his way; she had always found him so, in spite of herself. Maybe she could get fond enough of him for something more to develop.

But no. The time for that had been a year ago, when she first started looking for someone to get her pregnant, not now, when she had rejected Mike and found someone else who was better. Mike might make a good father, but that wasn't what she wanted him for, not entirely anyway.

For the other thing, for the warmth in the bed, the cuddles in the morning, the conversation over supper, she wanted someone else. Yet Owen (even if he had been available to her on a permanent basis) was totally unsuitable. She could hardly have found anyone less suitable. He would never have cuddled her, he wouldn't have sat with her in the evenings. He would be in the lab working, hunched over a desk, and in the mornings he would be cold, carrying his boxer shorts into the bathroom to take a quick shower and wash off any vestiges of their nights together. That was all she had known from Owen. There was no reason to expect anything else of him.

Everything was going according to plan. The plans just hadn't been complete enough.

CHAPTER TWENTY-THREE

After that revelation, Mike phoned Julia several times, but she always put him off calling in person. It wasn't because she didn't want to see him, simply because she thought he deserved better treatment. For once in her life, she was trying hard to be unselfish.

She hadn't intended to go to ante-natal classes this time round. Times had changed since she had Andrew, but not so much that the basic techniques of child-bearing needed to be re-learned. She went only for something to do to fill the time. The classes were taken by a health visitor called Mrs Holroyd, a thin, somehow scruffy-looking woman, who wore no make-up or stockings and whose hair needed a good trim. Julia rather liked her.

Julia felt she had little in common with the other mothers-to-be, who were mostly in their late teens or early twenties. One or two of them deemed it an achievement to light up a cigarette and finish smoking it while Mrs Holroyd was out of the room. Narrow horizons, thought Julia. Once she would have protested; now she didn't care about anyone else, as long as her own baby was born safely.

A girl of twenty or so, named Tracey, made an immediate attempt to befriend her. Tracey was grossly overweight, and should have had difficulty conceiving, but apparently she hadn't. Her food intake, which the dietician was attempting to help her regulate, was now her obsession, and she regaled Julia at every opportunity with full details of what she had eaten for each meal in the past three days. Talking about it was apparently her substitute for doing it. Looking as she did, Julia supposed it would have been unreasonable to suggest to her that she should have found some other interest in life rather than getting pregnant and lumbering herself with a child at an age where she had not begun to experience life. It was easy to imagine what Tracey's schooldays must have been like.

In her generosity, Tracey was ready to offer advice and assistance to Julia, whom she mistook for a first-time mother. She appeared slightly shocked when Julia confessed not only to being unmarried—Tracey was herself unmarried, after all—but to having no intention of getting married. However, the girl rallied quickly and launched into a series of naïve recommendations as to how Julia might better her situation. Grateful for not being required to do anything except nod occasionally in response, Julia reciprocated by taking Tracey to the café opposite the clinic afterwards for a cup of coffee and the pastry of her choice.

While they ate and drank, Tracey described her wedding plans in the kind of detail she normally reserved for her diet. The baby was due some time in December, and the wedding was to take place in February. Privately, Julia thought this was a little optimistic, but it seemed unkind to throw cold water on Tracey's grand ideas, so she made approving noises as Tracey explained how they were having the wedding ceremony at the registry office and the reception at a local hotel, one which Julia and Keith wouldn't have been able to afford at that age. Julia wondered where the money was coming from for all this, but it seemed settled. Tracey and her boyfriend, one Gavin, had of course intended to marry *before* having children, but it hadn't quite turned out as planned, and now they were "over the moon" at the idea of becoming parents, despite the fact that Gavin, or "Gav" as Tracey preferred to call him, was only nineteen, even younger than Tracey herself, or "Trace", as Gav allegedly called her.

Julia lasted for three ante-natal classes before the boredom got too much. She kept up her clinic visits, but anything else seemed an unnecessary chore. There was no one she could relate to at the classes—unless you counted Mrs Holroyd—and there was very little she could learn apart from renewing her acquaintance with relaxation techniques, which were best practised alone.

"Am I a snob," she wondered, "or am I just maladjusted, damaged beyond repair, unable to form relationships or communicate with other human beings?"

Christmas was drawing near again. There would be no invitation from the Grants this year, not that Julia could have accepted it in any case. They had heard about her pregnancy. Her mother had telephoned them to break the news. Julia couldn't face it, yet she felt they had some kind of right to know, though logic proclaimed otherwise. Mum claimed they didn't sound shocked, but who could tell? Apparently they wished Julia every health and happiness. She would hardly have expected them to say what they were really thinking, even to a third party, and she imagined that they had talked about her afterwards in less than glowing terms.

She couldn't have gone up there in her condition, even if they had asked. It was too close to full-term, and would have called for precisely the kind of exertion she needed to avoid. Miscarriage wasn't a real risk now, but she still couldn't afford to take chances. The waiting was the worst part of every pregnancy, as Julia now vividly recalled. It was the time when you could still enjoy yourself, but didn't want to. You could still go places, because you carried the baby everywhere with you. In a few weeks, you would miss this privilege, but right now you didn't want it. You just wanted it all over with. Julia especially wanted it, after all she had been through. In view of her threatened miscarriage, she had hoped that the doctor would suggest a Caesarean or at least take her in early. Unfortunately, she had been put on the books of a progressive obstetrician, one who believed in letting nature take its course. "You're healthy enough," they kept saying at the hospital. "Just take it easy."

Christmas Day. Julia sat at her mother's big dining table, unable to eat more than a meagre portion of turkey because of her tendency to heartburn. As for pudding, that was out of the question.

Rebecca, Gordon and Jack were with Gordon's parents this year. Jack was sitting up already, holding his own drinking beaker. For his Christmas meal, he would be having mashed-up turkey, mashed-up potato and mashed-up peas, followed by mashed-up ice cream. They phoned immediately after lunch.

"Have you opened all your presents?" Julia heard Mum say, and knew by the high-pitched, idiotic tone of her voice that she was trying to hold a conversation with her grandson, who could only make gurgling noises. He, at the other end of the line, probably wasn't even holding the receiver the right way up.

Eventually it was her own turn to talk to them, or at least to Becky.

"How's it going?" she asked, using their private voice.

"Wonderful." Julia knew that Gordon or his parents must be within earshot, otherwise Becky would probably have said, "Not too bad."

"Had any good presents?"

"Some lovely things, yes. Thanks for the cardigan, by the way. And Jack thanks you for the activity centre. He's playing with it right now."

There was a muffled interruption in the background.

"Oh yes, and Gordon says thanks for the computer games. He can't wait to play them."

"That's okay. Thanks for all your presents too." They had given Julia a matching nightie and dressing gown, roomy and eminently suitable for wearing in hospital. She nevertheless looked forward to being able to wear things that were not roomy again.

Funny how, when you weren't pregnant, you couldn't imagine what it was like to be pregnant, but when you *were* pregnant, you couldn't remember what it was like to be normal. Gradually it came back to Julia, when she started expanding. It always made her wonder how really fat people manage, tying their shoelaces, picking things up off the floor, so many other little tasks for which you need a normal-sized stomach. For girls like Tracey, pregnancy probably wouldn't make a noticeable difference.

Tracey had probably had her baby by now. With a shock, Julia realised, mid-conversation, that she was having contractions, and had been having them for the last hour or so.

"…don't you think?" Becky's voice wafted out of the distance into Julia's right ear.

"Sorry, what?" There was no need to panic. Perhaps she was imagining things.

"Never mind. I was just rambling. Are the parents bearing up okay?"

"Mum and Dad? They're champion, as Granddad Bill would have said. At least, they seem okay. I stayed here last night."

"I know. Mum told me. Was it awful?"

"No, actually it was much better than being in the house on my own. I didn't wake up till eight. Mind you, I'd been awake during the night."

"How come?"

"Not excitement over it being Christmas. To tell you the truth, I forgot what day it was. No, I just couldn't sleep. I was uncomfortable. I've got into a comfy position in my own bed, and it was strange being somewhere else. I never sleep all that well, in any case."

"It's a bummer, isn't it?" A strange expression for Becky to use. She couldn't be picking up slang off Jack, not just yet. Other mothers at the nursery, perhaps.

"How's Jack getting on at nursery?"

"Not bad. It's a bit of stimulation for him. I have to keep an eye out in case the toddlers trample on him without noticing, but I think he sort of gets something out of it. He takes everything in."

"Any sign of teeth yet?" Anything to prolong the conversation and avoid concentrating on herself.

"He keeps putting his fist in his mouth and dribbling, but I can't feel anything coming through. All the books say he should have started teething by now."

"Don't worry about it. The later he gets them, the longer they'll last. So some people say."

"Did...?" Becky was obviously about to ask about Julia's own experience with the boys, but it was still a taboo subject, in spite of everything. "What do *you* think?" she asked instead.

"Just don't worry. The doctor'll soon tell you if there's anything wrong."

Was that it, that twinge, was that the beginning of another contraction? Julia held her breath.

"I'd better go now. Gordon's waving at me frantically. There must be something on TV. Bye. Love to Mum and Dad."

"Bye, Becky. See you soon."

Gasping for air, she put down the receiver and returned her attention to her body, specifically the muscular contraction that was definitely in progress. There was no pain. It was ridiculous that she couldn't even remember what it felt like.

Returning to the living room, she sat down on one of the hard chairs and attempted to resume normal conversation with her parents.

"Becky sounds well. They seem to be having a great time there."

"Oh, good." Her mother barely took her eyes off Bruce Forsyth, but her father turned to look at her.

"Are you okay, love?"

"Fine. How about that drop of sherry? I didn't feel like it earlier, but I do now. Just the tiniest glass." Anything to take her mind off the contractions, if that was what they were. Sherry might relax her just enough.

Her father couldn't disguise his surprise.

"Of course, love. Eileen, sherry?"

"No thanks. I don't want to be getting drunk. That wine we had with the meal was enough for me."

Julia had declined the "wine" and every other alcoholic drink offered her over the festive season, but at this moment she needed calming.

During the afternoon and evening of seasonal television programmes that lay ahead, she would try to sit still and not show her parents that anything was happening. She didn't want to alarm them. On the other hand, if the baby was coming, she ought to walk up and down to help it along. That would only alert their suspicions, though. Better to sit tight and relax. It would be ages yet.

What a day to have a baby. This kind of thing only happened to other people, those lucky women who lie in hospital listening to Christmas carollers and have their photo taken for the paper. It was too good to be true.

The new next-door neighbours called at about four. Marcia and Allan, they were called: a youngish couple with children. The children didn't accompany them, they were out playing on their new bikes. Julia had never met Marcia and Allan before, but she could tell they knew all about her by the way they studiously avoided any reference to husbands, families, death, suicide or pregnancy. Admittedly, apart from the first two, most of those things were unlikely to crop up in a normal Christmas Day conversation, but there was still an awkwardness about their manner towards her that told its own tale.

Marcia and Allan stayed for nearly an hour. Julia made the most of the opportunity to walk around and change position frequently, in the hope of bringing labour closer, but when they were gone, she realised sadly that the contractions had stopped. No Christmas Day baby after all, and perhaps it was just as well. She had always felt sorry for those children, only getting one present a year from most people.

It was late when she gave in and went to bed. Mum and Dad were only staying up for her sake, she knew. None of them had been able to help brooding on those Christmases past, times when the boys had been given particular presents or had made something at school. Those cardboard angels and lopsided calendars that had to be put on display. She tried not to throw them away until they were well and truly broken and useless. Sometimes Andrew would find something in the box, when he was helping her decorate the tree, and would say, "Where did this come from?" not remembering that he had made it himself a year or two previously. When that happened, she would know it was safe to get rid of it, though she didn't always do so, not if it was something she found particularly charming or had become fond of.

"Do you remember that reindeer Keith and Andrew made a couple of years ago?" she asked suddenly, in the middle of the Christmas edition of Mum's favourite sitcom.

Mum and Dad looked startled.

"I remember," said Dad slowly. "It had gold antlers." His eyes glistened with unshed tears.

"Made of that crinkly stuff. And one of them kept slipping down."

"Andrew was crying because he couldn't get it to stay on, and I glued it for him, but it wasn't in the right position."

"I think it's still there, in the house somewhere." The truth was, she had been afraid to go through the box of decorations. For the second year running, she hadn't put up a tree or anything else at home. Next year would be different.

CHAPTER TWENTY-FOUR

Julia woke. Something. A searing pain. A pain she recognised. Like the worst of the periods she had had in her college days. A pain that turned to an ache, then back to a pain.

"Ow!" she gasped, and tried to lie still.

The pain subsided. She rolled onto her side, panting, and looked at the clock. It was three in the morning. She breathed deeply, and tried to sit up.

And already the pain was coming again. Julia almost fell out of bed, crouching on all fours. It was a good position, but it couldn't take the pain away.

"Oh, my God!" she said aloud, but quietly. She had forgotten how bad it could be. Crippling.

When it had departed again, she sat back on her knees, sweating, and picked up her watch. Five minutes, or less, between contractions.

There wasn't any time to waste. This was the real thing. Pulling on a dressing gown, she staggered to the bathroom to relieve herself. Everything came out in a rush. The pain was on its way back, before she even had time to flush the toilet. Holding herself up with her hands on the cistern, she looked into the bowl. Blood. She reached for the bathroom cabinet. Was it safe to take painkillers? She couldn't see any.

Supporting herself against the wall, she made her way to her parents' room. There was a light on.

"Julia, is that you?" she heard her mother call out.

"Mum! I need to…I think it's coming."

Suddenly the landing light was on, and both her parents were standing there, confused, her father's hair—what little he had left—standing on end. He must have thrown on his pyjama jacket, because it wasn't done up straight. Funny how you could notice little things like that at a time like this.

Julia's mother held her arm.

"Shall I help you back to bed?"

"No! It's time, Mum, it's coming. We need to go to hospital."

"Oh!" Her mother was panicking, as though she had never been through anything like this before. Of course, it would have been a long time, Julia thought absently, distracted from normal thought by the pain. Mum hadn't been there when Jeremy was born, nor Andrew, nor Jack. She only had her own experiences to go on, and the most recent of those was nearly forty years ago.

Even in her semi-incapacitated state, Julia could see that her father was confused, expecting Mum to know instinctively what was to be done.

"Dad, can you get the car out? Or call an ambulance or something? I need to go into hospital *now*."

He came back to life.

"I'll just get some shoes," he said, darting back into the bedroom.

"Mum," said Julia, "help me get a coat on, and some shoes, and put my overnight bag in the car."

Funny how she was the one giving orders at the critical moment, when she should probably have been letting everyone else do the thinking for her.

"Oh, Jesus!" she screamed, feeling the heat between her legs. "It's coming! I can feel it!"

Her father, hearing her screams, rushed back out to the landing.

"It's all right, love," he was saying. "It's all right. I'll carry you downstairs."

"Don't be ridiculous!" she shrieked. "Just help me walk!"

Somehow, seconds later, she found herself at the foot of the stairs, her father holding her up, her mother nowhere in sight now.

"What the hell are you doing up there, Eileen?" her father shouted, his anxiety manifesting itself as anger.

"I'm just getting her things," came her mother's tearful voice. "Get her into the car, and I'll be with you."

Then Julia was in the car, half-sitting, half-lying on the back seat, though she wasn't sure how she had got there.

The car journey passed without incident. Thank God it was three o'clock in the morning, she thought with what remained of her consciousness. Or maybe it was four o'clock by now. And the pain again. Could Dad drive all right? Please, God, don't let him jump any red lights.

The hospital was far enough, but they were there before she knew it.

"I thought we'd never get here!" she heard Mum exclaim.

"I drove as fast as I could, Eileen," came her father's voice, in reply. They both sounded far away.

Then there was a trolley, and a male orderly pushing her towards the delivery room. She guessed that it was the delivery room, but she didn't have time to notice the décor.

"Mrs Grant," said a nurse's voice. "Not due till January sixth."

"Julia?" said another nurse. "Julia? Bear up, dear, we're nearly there."

She had always hated how the nurses these days called you by your first name without so much as a by-your-leave. This probably wasn't the time to complain.

They were manhandling her onto a high bed, and there was anaesthetic around. She could smell it.

"Take the mask, dear," said the nurse who was on first-name terms. "Take the mask, Julia."

"Mum!" she shouted.

"I'm here, love. Don't worry." Her mother's voice floated down to her from a distance.

"Do you want your mum with you, Julia?" asked the nurse.

"Of course I bloody do!"

No time to notice how Mum looked. Frantic, no doubt, but there was nothing Julia could do about it. She couldn't even help herself. Mum's hand in hers, gripping tightly.

The gas and air, coming through the mask into her nose and mouth, made her feel even more dopey, but the pain was still there.

"Fully dilated," commented a nurse. Midwife, Julia corrected herself internally. Her thoughts were coherent still. A Boxing Day baby.

"This is like an episode of Corrie," she said to her mother.

"What, love?"

"They always have their babies at stupid times, and in stupid places. But they never have them in hospital, do they? Always in the backs of taxis, or…ow!"

"Yes, love." She knew her mother didn't understand a word. Was she rambling, or did it make perfect sense?

Phone Owen. He should be here. Julia gripped the rail of the bed as another cloud of pain passed over.

"Phone him," she said half-heartedly.

"What?" Mum's voice was anxious, but her face was out of the line of vision. Phoning him would be pointless. He didn't even know he was the child's father.

She could feel the bulge between her legs, like the urge to go to the toilet after a big meal, only not the same.

"Your waters haven't broken, Julia," said one of the nurses. Midwives. "I'm going to do it for you, okay? Because Baby's ready to come and we don't want to hold him up, do we?"

A vague memory surfaced. This had happened before, with Jeremy, or was it Andrew? One of the children that no longer existed.

She felt nothing, only a burning space between her legs.

"Now push, Julia."

"Push, come on, push."

"Now stop pushing."

Make up your bloody mind, she thought. Mustn't swear in front of Mum, mustn't.

"Here's Baby's head. Can you feel it?"

The joy, oh the joy, as she felt the downy head of a baby between her legs for the third and last time in her life. She could remember, almost, she thought, the same thing with Andrew, believing totally that it was the last time she would ever feel it.

Mum was crying too.

"The baby's coming!" she exclaimed, between her tears.

"I know," said Julia, in a voice audible only to herself.

"One more push, now."

Julia remembered how to do it. Follow through, she told herself. Follow through. Barely conscious. Barely aware of what was happening. She followed through.

"Excellent."

"Well done, Julia."

"Oh, the baby!" That was her mother.

"It's a little girl," said the midwife, holding it up for her to see before placing it on her tummy.

Blinking in the light, the child looked her mother in the face. She looked just like Owen.

CHAPTER TWENTY-FIVE

The baby was perfect. She had ten tiny fingers, ten tiny toes, a red, scrunched face, and eyes that looked around the room a lot.

"She's been here before," commented the midwife.

The child's hair, plastered to her little head at first, and then, after her bath, fluffy and fair, was not like either of the boys' hair, which had been coarse and dark at the beginning. She reminded Julia only vaguely of her previous babies. Thank God.

Now, a silent nurse was giving Julia a bed bath. The soothing coolness of the flannel was a sensation she recalled only distantly from her previous deliveries, but was nevertheless another reminder. Then there was the journey, by trolley, from the delivery room to the maternity ward. A real mother once again, she lay motionless on her back, enjoying the ride with the new viewpoint on the world which it gave, moving her head from time to time, just enough to see the baby, in its little mobile cot, being wheeled alongside her by the nurse. The lift arrived and two other nurses got out, pausing to admire the new arrival. You would have thought the novelty would have worn off for them, but they sounded for all the world as if they thought this the prettiest child they had seen during the whole of their careers. As they were both only in their mid-twenties, Julia reflected, perhaps they hadn't seen all that many babies. Perhaps it was always a relief to see a new, healthy one, in place of the dead ones, deformed ones, handicapped ones they must, occasionally, be faced with.

There was satisfaction, but also pain, in no longer being a make-believe mother.

"All right, love?" asked the young orderly, matter-of-factly, as an involuntary tear trickled down Julia's cheek. Looking up into his face, she could tell that he was only slightly concerned. New mothers always cry. After all, it is the happiest moment of their lives. For Julia, that was true ten times over.

Incredibly, the time of the baby's birth was registered as five twenty-five, and it was eight o'clock before Julia found herself ensconced in her room, away from all the noise and fuss, being offered a breakfast that had genuine appeal. She was ravenous. The rest of the day passed in a daze, punctuated by an almost continuous stream of visitors—mainly Mum and Dad leaving and returning, but other people came too. In the evening, she was surprised, and even pleased, to see Edie, who presented her with a little package in unpleasant green wrapping paper, which, when opened, turned out to contain the promised white matinee jacket and matching bootees.

The Mayberrys' congratulatory card was added to others from the family that had made an appearance on the bedside table. Julia recalled another occasion, in another hospital, when a nurse had made her take her two cards off the bedside tray because it was needed for another "new mum" in the same ward (whose own tray was too full of cards to be used). There were no other mothers in this room.

The real tiredness did not set in until next day. That was the way it was, Julia remembered. Being tired as you had never known tiredness before. She had been through hell with the boys, stuck in a four-bedded ward with other women whose babies slept while hers cried and cried while hers slept. She knew Keith would have approved of her spending money on a private room, now that she had it. There was nothing she valued more than the privacy, being able to take your baby out of her cot and nurse her when you felt like it, have visitors when you felt like it, and not worry about the disturbing the other mothers.

Hospital was, nevertheless, purgatory.

Julia had never had much success with breast-feeding before, and she made only a cursory attempt this time, putting the baby on the bottle that very first night so that she needn't be woken. A certain amount of guilt accompanied this decision, as though she had wished very hard for something, been given it, and now did not want it. Her little girl was a chance to do the things right that she had done wrong the previous time—the previous two times. But the mistake with Jeremy and Andrew had not been the decision to stop breast-feeding, it had been all the soul-searching that went with it. She had made herself ill with worry. All the publicity, the suggestion that it might be linked with cot death, and so on. The boys had been a picture of health, always, and her daughter would be no different. Only this time she would be healthy herself too, and better able to take care of her child.

Sleepily, Julia planned the meals she would prepare for herself when she got home, full of vitamins and fibre and protein. She pictured the kitchen cupboards in a few months' time, full of little jars of the best baby food—milk puddings, apple puree, macaroni cheese.

She couldn't get off to sleep properly, but lay much of the time in a kind of doze, daydreaming about what was to come and what had already been, sometimes thinking of the baby and her future and then allowing her mind to wander until a picture of Owen's lithe, pale body strayed into her field of thought. Then she would stop, sit up, read a magazine, take a little walk to the window and back, which was as far as her stitches would allow her to go in comfort. It would probably take longer to heal up, this time, because she was so much older.

It would be a relief to get home. At least there she could do as she liked, although she would still have to endure the daily visits from doctors and health visitors for a while. It was probably necessary, for some people, the sixteen-year-olds living in council flats with boyfriends called Darren, but it irritated her that they couldn't see how different she, Julia Grant, was from the average unmarried mother, or indeed the average mother, and how well able to take care of herself.

Actually, she realised, even as she was thinking it, that wasn't true. She wasn't that good at taking care of herself. She'd proved that in the last year and a half, if anyone ever had. Social Services shouldn't trust a woman with her history to look after a baby. That flood of panic flowed over her again as she thought of the months and years ahead, caring for that little girl, that innocent.

Imogen. Innogen was the original name, from one of Shakespeare's plays. When they copied the manuscript, centuries ago, someone misread it and it became the name Imogen. Poor old Imogen in the play didn't have much fun, although she ended up still alive, which was more than could be said for a lot of the other characters.

The name had planted itself in her mind months ago, but Julia hadn't thought seriously about it, or any other name, because she didn't want to count her chickens. It could have been another boy; in fact, she realised she had been almost assuming that it would be a boy, because clearly there was a propensity for boys in her family, in Keith's family, that is. Owen had a sister though, and it was all to do with the sperm.

She was so glad, now that she considered it properly, that she should have been given a daughter. There would be reminders of Jeremy and Andrew, naturally, but they wouldn't be half as strong with a little girl, a little girl called Imogen.

Now, and only now, did Julia re-experience, in full, glorious and painful detail, what it had been like with Jeremy, when she had first had him. Such perfection in one small creature. The love was overwhelming, it devoured all her senses. There was no respite from it. Even when the baby cried and she was so tired she could have hurled the little body against the wall to silence it, she still loved it—loved Imogen—more than anything in the world, enough to die for, enough to kill for, and easily enough to give up any man for.

"Will your husband be coming in to see the baby today?" asked a bright young nurse as she tidied Julia's bed. "Does he know he can come any time? We don't have visiting hours for new dads."

She must be pretty new, Julia thought. Even if they weren't able to give staff warnings about individual patients, there were always bound to be one or two women around who didn't conform to the ideal of the nuclear family.

"I'm not married," said Julia.

The nurse froze in mid-tidy. But of course, Julia reasoned, they must have taken her to be a respectable married woman, carrying the title of "Mrs Grant".

"My husband died," she explained.

This only made things worse. "Oh, I'm sorry," stammered the nurse, obviously assuming that the late Mr Grant had managed to father the child before his untimely demise.

"No, I mean, he died some time ago. About two years ago, actually." It shocked her to use the words. Two years. She double-checked her dates. Yes, it was nearly two years. "The father's someone else. And he won't be coming."

The nurse made an excuse to leave the room quickly. Left alone, Julia found that she was not disturbed by the incident. On the contrary, it was rather refreshing to find someone who didn't know her circumstances. At least it proved that they weren't all out there talking about her after all.

Apart from these occasional visits from individual nurses, the hospital was cold and unfriendly. Julia ventured out of her private room only when there was no alternative. There were no complications, and consequently there was no need for her to remain there for more than a couple of days. She had a television in her room, but seldom switched it on. Outside, on the wards and in the corridors, she could hear the voices of other new mothers, some of them quiet and anxious, others coarse and strident. The nurses likewise.

One voice seemed strikingly familiar. Julia was curious enough to put her head outside the door, to witness Tracey, her former acquaintance from ante-natal classes, trudging along the corridor in a voluminous dressing-gown, wheeling a cot alongside her.

"Tracey!" exclaimed Julia, genuinely pleased to see a familiar face. "Is this your baby? May I look?"

The baby, a boy, was large and ugly, but looked contented enough. Tracey herself displayed no particular pleasure in him, or in seeing Julia again, but stood sullenly by the cot as Julia expressed insincere admiration for his robustness.

"And you, Tracey," she added, beginning to feel uncomfortable, "how are you?"

"I had to have a Caesarean," said Tracey. "You know, where they cut you open. I got to stay in here for a week because of that. I only just got up. I'll be out the day after tomorrow, though."

"How are the wedding plans coming along? Everything okay?"

"No," replied Tracey. "We…um…we're not getting married now."

Seeing that she was close to tears, Julia made Tracey come inside and sit on the easy chair in her room.

"Tell me about it," said Julia. If she was going to persevere with life, she might as well try to help others besides herself and Imogen.

"Gav says he's not ready for the responsibility," muttered Tracey. "So we're not going to get married just yet. Or maybe not at all. It's for the best. I understand how he feels."

Of course you do, Julia thought. You feel just the same yourself, just as unready, only you're the one stuck with the kid and you've got to go through with it. If the truth be told, Tracey was better off without Gav, but there would be no way to make her understand that.

"Oh dear," said Julia, trying to sound caring, modelling herself on Nora Penhaligon. "How will you manage, then? Are your parents able to help?"

"I'm going to live with Mum and Dad for the time being," said Tracey without enthusiasm, "then I'm going to see if I can get a council flat. That'll be the best thing, won't it?"

She was looking to Julia for guidance.

"Will it?" Julia replied. "Are your parents happy to have you with them? If they are, I should stay there as long as you can, because you need support when you've got a child."

"Oh, Gav will support me," protested Tracey. "He said so. He's going to give me so much a week out of his wages, and he's going to come and see us every weekend."

"Every weekend? That's not very often for the baby to see his father." Julia restrained herself from saying what she really thought, that they would probably be better off not seeing Gav at all.

"Well…I thought that at first. But perhaps it's for the best. I don't want Gav to feel tied down. Mum says he'll never marry me if I make it too easy for him, but I think he will. I'm sure he will."

Julia said nothing.

"Don't you think so?" Tracey probed.

"I don't know. I haven't met Gavin, so I can hardly judge."

Tracey sat quietly for a moment, gently pushing the cot with the sleeping baby in it to and fro a few inches at a time.

"I wish I was like you, Julia," she said at last.

"No, Tracey, you don't. If you knew what I've been through to have this baby…" It would be easy to tell Tracey everything, to obtain her horrified sympathy and leave her thinking how well off she was, but that would help neither of them.

"Tracey, you're young," she continued. "Things will come right in time. I'll give you my phone number. If I can ever help you, get in touch with me. In the meantime…"

She reached for her handbag.

"I don't want to offend you, but can I give you some money? For the baby," she added as an afterthought.

Tracey looked nervous. "There's no need."

"Of course there is. You've got a little boy to bring up. You need to be able to get him things."

There was about sixty pounds in her purse. She counted out fifty, rolled up the notes and pushed them at Tracey.

"Take this."

Tracey held the notes in her palm and looked at them in awe, without unrolling them to see how much she was being offered. She looked into Julia's face, as though frightened that it was some kind of joke.

"Thank you," she said.

After Tracey had gone, Julia thought she should have felt pleased with herself. Instead, she felt drained and somehow dissatisfied.

What Tracey had sought from her was emotional support and maybe some good advice. Julia had fobbed her off with money, not even enough money to buy a decent pushchair. She thought of calling her back and offering her more, writing a cheque perhaps. The embarrassment factor was what stopped her, but there was logic behind it. It simply wasn't enough. No money was enough to compensate for Tracey's disappointment. She would go through life suffering similar disappointments, and barely complaining. Julia could do nothing for Tracey, just as she could do nothing for herself.

CHAPTER TWENTY-SIX

"What are you going to call her?" asked Julia's mother. It was her way of asking who the father was.

Julia sighed. "I haven't quite decided. I thought of Imogen. What do you think?"

"Unusual," said her mother, after a slight hesitation that conveyed doubt. "How did you come to think of that?"

That was her way of asking if Julia had discussed it with the baby's father.

"It just came to mind. I liked it. But I'll have to think about it a bit more, before I decide for certain."

"Oh, by the way, that friend of yours phoned. What's his name now?"

For an awful second, she thought Mum had found them out. But it couldn't have been Owen, since he didn't know anything about the baby, not even that it existed.

"I don't know who you mean."

"You know. Keith's partner, the one who was so good. It's not a proper name, it's initials, P-something. I can never remember."

"You mean PJ."

"That's the one. He said he'll call to see you. He's such a kind person."

Sitting alone later, nursing a sleepy Imogen, Julia wondered whether perhaps she ought to have consulted Owen about the naming of their child. It would be asking for trouble, and yet it somehow seemed the decent thing to do. It wasn't as if he had *chosen* to have nothing to do with the baby. She hadn't given him that choice.

There had been several odd moments when she had wanted to phone him, if only to hear his voice. He had a right to know that the child had been born—but no doubt he would find out via the college grapevine before too long. Besides, she intended to ask Mum to put the birth in the local paper, just as soon as the name was definite, and then everyone would know.

On the whole, it was lucky that she couldn't easily get to a telephone.

It was in the evening that Rebecca arrived, quite unexpectedly. Julia hadn't thought of seeing her until at least the following day. There were hugs, and tears, and all the things there should have been but probably wouldn't have been if everything had been normal.

"Mum tells me you're thinking of Imogen as a name," said Becky, looking down tenderly at the baby girl. "I *love* it."

"Do you, really? I don't think Mum does."

Becky smiled and sighed. "She wanted a royal name—Elizabeth or Sarah or Diana, something like that."

"I was thinking of Alexandra as a middle name. I wonder if that would do her."

"Mmm." Rebecca's mind was already somewhere else, as she gazed transfixed at her new niece.

"Not broody again already, surely?" Julia allowed herself the luxury of a laugh.

Rebecca looked up. "Oh, sorry. No, I was just thinking what a miracle it is. Both of us mothers."

"You're a mother. I'm a one-parent family."

"Oh, go on."

There was a silence. The question was forming itself.

"Look, Julia, I know it's none of my business, and I didn't want to ask you before, just in case—well, just in case. But now that she's born and she's lovely and healthy, will you tell me if it's what I think it is?"

"If what's what you think what is?"

Rebecca stroked the bedcover, still staring into the cot. "Was it artificial insemination?"

Julia didn't answer.

"Okay, you don't have to tell me. I just wondered."

"Why? What difference does it make to anything?"

"I knew you'd think I was just being nosey." There were tears in Becky's eyes now. "But it's not that. You've always been my friend as well as my sister. I just wanted to know if you were all right. I mean, if you'd been hurt."

Julia felt wretched.

"The answer's no." Even as she said it, she knew it wasn't true.

"You're right," she continued, in an effort to make both of them feel better. "I used someone to get the baby. He went along with it. He knew why I was doing it. We didn't have any sort of relationship. Other than sexual. And I won't see him again."

There was a long silence, during which Rebecca stared at the baby while digesting the information.

"I see," she said at last. "Okay. I can see why you wouldn't want Mum and Dad to know, but the trouble is, not knowing might be making it worse. They're thinking all sorts of things."

"I can't help that. I've got a responsibility to him, as well. I don't want anyone to find out what he did for me."

"I don't suppose it's anyone I know?" It was the nearest Becky could have come to asking the question outright.

"You don't know him." At least Julia could feel she was telling the truth, for once.

After Rebecca had left, Julia stared for a long time at the sleeping child. It seemed so long ago that she had gone through all this with the boys, so long that she had forgotten the feelings and the experiences. Even now, it didn't seem at all familiar.

To be a mother again, that was the amazing thing. To feel responsible for someone else. The fear that went with it was exactly the same as when she had been in her twenties, she remembered that much. Perhaps now it was greater, because she had no one to support her when things got rough. Mum and Dad, of course,

Becky, of course. But no one who would be there, in the house, with her and Imogen. No one who could take the baby when it was crying and give Julia a rest.

At the moment, she felt she didn't want anyone and didn't need any help. It might be different in a few days time, though. What about next month, or next year? Could she still manage on her own then?

There were a few cards in the morning. Her mother had picked up the post from the house, and there had been three pushed through the door as well, including a couple from neighbours. The last envelope had her name scrawled on it in handwriting she didn't immediately recognise.

Her hand started to tremble as she read the greeting.

"Best wishes, Owen and Jenny."

She looked at it several times without believing it.

"Who's that one from?" asked Mum eventually, when Julia had held it for several minutes without speaking.

"Erm…some people I know from the college." She put it down on the bedspread, knowing that her mother would immediately pick it up to look at.

"Owen and Jenny," she read out loud. "Do I know them?"

"I don't think so, Mum. He's a lecturer at the college."

"Oh, that's nice of him." Mum laughed. "I expect his wife had to remind him to send it, though."

Julia tried to smile.

"I was wondering how they knew."

"I expect they saw it in the paper," said her mother matter-of-factly.

Julia was stunned. "You put it in the paper?"

"Of course." Mum looked suddenly anxious. "You don't mind, do you? You know I've always…I put Jack in for Rebecca and Gordon, you know that."

"Yes, but…"

"Oh dear, I'm sorry. It was thoughtless, wasn't it? I suppose you didn't want people to know."

"No, Mum, it's not that. It's only…I thought you'd be ashamed."

Her mother's expression changed.

"Ashamed?" Her voice had grown quite loud. "Ashamed of my own grandchild? Do I have any reason to be ashamed?"

Julia shook her head, and looked away.

It was a few moments before she realised that her mother was crying.

"What's the matter, Mum?" she asked, unnecessarily. "I'm sorry, I didn't mean to upset you."

Mum was crying too much to make any sense, when she did attempt to explain herself. Julia knew full well what was upsetting her, and regretted the words she had used. Her parents were, in all truth, embarrassed and distressed by the fact that she had become pregnant without being married, but their concern had been chiefly for Julia herself, and the implication that they were not proud of their granddaughter was too much to be borne. Why hadn't she seen that from the beginning?

"Please, Mum, don't cry. It was a stupid thing to say. I meant that you were ashamed of *me*, not of Imogen. And I only meant, because you care about me. I know I've let you down—I feel I've let you down—by what I've done. I just didn't expect that you would put it in the paper, at least not yet. But I don't mind. I'm glad you cared enough to do it. Please stop crying now."

She had tried to put a comforting arm around her mother's shoulders, insofar as she could do so while still holding the baby. Mum had stopped crying now, but was still wiping her eyes with a crumpled tissue.

"I'm sorry, love. I shouldn't be so silly. Only I've been very anxious, you know, about you and Rebecca. And I'm so relieved that you're both well and have beautiful children. You can't imagine what it's been like."

After her mother had gone, Julia reflected again on how selfish she had been. She had known that her parents were going through hell, almost as much as she was herself. In a way, it was worse for them. They still grieved for the boys and missed them. The way they refrained from mentioning them was merely proof of this, meaning that they couldn't trust themselves not to break down.

Julia herself had loaded more anxiety on them by her suicide attempt. Then it was Becky and her untimely pregnancy. Then Julia herself again, getting pregnant at forty-two, by some anonymous man, and announcing that she was going to bring up the child alone. Rarely had she stopped to think about what they were suffering. But then, if she had, it would have been too much to take.

At home with Imogen, Julia alternated between basking in the attention she was getting and feeling oddly dissatisfied. The baby took up a lot of time, but she had always known how it would be. It was no piece of cake, being a mother. If it hadn't been easy first time round, it was hardly likely to be any easier now.

There were plenty of congratulatory phone calls, and a few personal callers. One of the first was Linda. After giving PJ's apologies for non-attendance, she made the usual approving noises, then sat in silence, waiting for Julia to bring up the other subject.

"How are things now, with you and PJ?," asked Julia, dutifully. "Is everything all right?"

"Actually," Linda began in a conspiratorial tone, "it seems I got it wrong. There wasn't anyone. I tackled him about it, and he assured me it was all in my imagination."

Oh yeah.

"That's all right then." What would be the point in asking Linda whether she believed him? If she didn't, then she obviously didn't want Julia to know. If she did, there was no reason to plant doubts in her mind. Ignorance is bliss.

Linda didn't stay long, and Julia knew that she had come only to talk about her own situation, to reassure herself by telling Julia, or maybe to make sure Julia was convinced and wouldn't mention it to anyone else. The baby present was a generous one, though. PJ could well afford it, but it was nice all the same. All these things that people were giving her for Imogen, Julia cherished them all. Soft, pastel-coloured cot blankets, brilliantly white towels with satin trim, little dresses, quite impractical but so pretty, and all the more delightful for being something she had never been given the first time and second time around.

Mum and Dad were there next morning, as usual, talking about christenings, which she didn't want to think about yet. A double christening, with Jack, who had not yet been "done", was suggested, but it posed logistical problems—"Which church?" They could hardly expect Julia to take Imogen up to Norfolk just to be christened.

Julia's mother answered the phone and passed it to her.

"Hello, Julia." He didn't need to say who it was. She got up and went into the hall, closing the door.

"Owen? How… How nice to hear from you."

"Do you know why I've rung?"

"No," she lied. "I suppose you heard about the baby."

"I sent you a card."

It had slipped her mind. "Yes, of course, I got it. Thanks."

"Is there anything you want to tell me?"

She hesitated. "Like what?"

"When I saw you in March, you said you were already pregnant."

"And?"

"You weren't, were you? It's mine, isn't it?"

"What makes you think that?"

"I can add up. If it's not mine, it's the longest bloody pregnancy on bloody record. I should have known you were lying to me."

"Would it have made any difference?"

He put the phone down without replying.

CHAPTER TWENTY-SEVEN

"I suppose I shouldn't be surprised to see you," she said, trying to make her voice as cold and unwelcoming as she could. "I might have known you wouldn't be able to keep your promise."

Owen's face began to turn red.

"It's not quite like that, Julia," he said. "Yes, I admit, I wanted to see the baby, but mainly I've come just to check that you were all right. I suppose that's allowed, isn't it? I suppose I'm allowed to care about you?"

"We agreed," she said curtly.

"When we said we wouldn't see each other again, I didn't think that meant we would go out of our way to avoid one another."

"No, okay," she accepted grudgingly.

"Well, then?"

"You want to see her?"

"No. I want to see *you*. I want you to tell me that you're all right. And then, if you want to, you can show me *your* baby."

"I'm all right. Do you want a coffee? The baby's sleeping at the moment."

It was starting all over again, and she couldn't stop herself. Even now, in the morning, even here in the kitchen, she wanted him.

"How's Jenny?" she asked spitefully.

He didn't reply.

She poured the coffee into the mugs, stirring his. A sudden, terrible thought struck her.

"You haven't told her, have you?"

"No," he said curtly.

"Thank God for that." She wasn't sure why she was being quite so nasty to him. There was no reason not to believe his explanation for being here.

"So?" she prompted.

"So what?"

"So how is she, then?"

He still didn't respond, but stood looking into the mug she had handed him, as though it contained some foreign beverage he had never seen before.

"Do we have to talk about Jenny?" he said at last.

Julia shrugged.

"I want to know if *you're* all right," he said again.

She gestured towards herself.

"As you see, Owen. Hardly any sign left."

"Good." He didn't smile.

There was something not quite right about him. He was here to see the baby, but that wasn't all. His face was drawn.

"Is something wrong, Owen? You look…anxious."

He muttered something she didn't catch.

"What's that?"

He raised his voice and spoke slowly and deliberately. "I said I've lost my job."

She didn't know how to react. "You've lost your job? Why? How? What happened?"

"Made redundant. Cutbacks. You know."

"Oh God, Owen, I'm sorry. But you won't have any difficulty getting another one, surely?"

"Maybe not." He looked unimpressed by her encouragement. "It's a blow, though. Not the kind of thing you'd understand, I don't suppose."

The rancour shouldn't have surprised her.

"Can I do anything for you?" He knew she had money. Was that why he was here?

"Like what?" No, she had been wrong, he wasn't looking for a pay-off. She couldn't make him a direct offer without starting another argument.

"If you took my car, you could sell yours. Would that be any help?"

"What would I tell Jenny?"

"Tell her the truth. Tell her you were given it by a mad woman. Tell her you did some odd jobs for me and I gave you the car as payment. Tell her anything you like."

"As it happens," he said sourly, "I don't have to tell her anything."

Julia surmised what had happened. He *had* told Jenny after all, she had gone off the deep end, and they had split up. Something like that.

"How did she find out? Did you tell her?" she asked after a long pause.

Owen, clearly mystified, shrugged.

"If you're thinking she knows about…"—he gestured vaguely to the space between them—"about *this*, you're wrong. I already said I haven't told her. She's left me for someone else. I don't think she's coming back."

He looked as if he was going to cry.

"When did this happen?"

"About three weeks ago."

So he hadn't come running straight to Julia.

"Do you want to talk about it?" was all she could think of to say.

"It was one of the lecturers on her BEd course, a bloke I knew quite well as it happens. I didn't have any idea. There were no clues, if you know what I mean. She said she never meant it to happen, but I suppose what she really meant was that she didn't mean for me to find out. But I did. Somebody else told me they'd seen them together, and then it all fell into place. I…"

"Drink some coffee," she said. "And for God's sake, sit down."

He did as he was told. Julia's own thoughts were in such disarray that she didn't know how to calm him. It was some time before he resumed talking.

"I went over his house. He's married, with kids, can you believe? We argued on the doorstep, and I punched him. That's how I got the sack."

"Hang on. You just said you were made redundant."

"Technically. I had to agree to it, or they'd have sacked me anyway and I'd never have got a reference. Let's face it, you can't have the teaching staff going round hitting lumps out of each other."

"But if he's married, how can Jenny move in with him?"

"No, he's moved in with her. In our flat. We worked something out. I'm in a bedsit."

"You're joking!" Under the circumstances, it was about the worst thing she could possibly have said. He looked up at her, eyes moist and red.

"I'm sorry," she pleaded. "I mean, it's so unbelievable, to treat you like that."

"Oh, is it?"

He was thinking of what they had done, she knew. The comparison was too close for comfort.

"I lied to her," he went on. "I cheated on her, I let her down. And all the time, I took her for granted. How should I expect to be treated?"

"That was different, Owen. You did what you did for the best reasons."

"The first time, maybe. But what about after? Or have you forgotten that there was an 'after'?"

Julia's face felt hot.

"Please don't blame me, Owen. I can't bring myself to regret it."

He said nothing. A weak cry came from the next room. The baby must have surfaced. Owen looked towards the door. Having emptied his coffee mug, he got up and placed it carefully in the sink.

"I want to see my daughter now," he said, his manner businesslike. "And then I'm going."

Without a word, she led him into the living room, where Imogen lay in her carry-cot, just woken. Julia lifted her out and cradled her.

Owen looked bemused. He put out a finger to touch Imogen's little nose.

"She's going to have red hair," he said.

"I think you're right. Do you want to hold her?"

He hesitated. "If that's okay," he said, standing awkwardly as if to brace himself for the impact of ten pounds of baby against his chest. When the exchange was completed, he stood looking down at her as if in wonder.

Imogen whimpered a little. Julia found her dummy, and stuck it in her mouth to comfort her.

"She'll probably want a feed in a minute. No, you're all right," she protested as Owen made to give the baby back.

"I never expected this," he said. "To see her like this, so real. I've never been interested in babies. But she's so...She even looks like—like *us*."

"I'm glad you think she's pretty."

He managed a smile. "At least something's turned out right in my rotten life," he said.

Momentarily shocked by the bitterness of his tone, Julia turned away. What to do now. It was bothering her. She could get entangled so easily. The temptation overcame her better instincts.

"Will you stay and have something to eat?"

"No, thanks. I think I should get off home—I mean back to where I'm staying."

He handed the baby back with tenderness. Picking up his jacket, he turned towards the door.

"Nothing's changed, has it?" he asked, without looking around.

Julia had no answer.

After he had gone, she found the tears starting to spring out again. She consoled herself by baring her breasts to Imogen. The feeding act gave her some satisfaction, even though she only did it once a day. It was amazing that she had managed to keep it up for so long.

Sleeping at night still wasn't easy. Already the baby slept through till about seven a.m., but it didn't make it easier for Julia to empty her mind, except when she was physically exhausted after a particularly taxing day. Now she had something else to think about.

She dreamed she had the boys back. They were there, in the living room, looking down at Imogen in her cot. Owen was there too. She was introducing him to the boys as "your new father".

"I don't like him," said Andrew, forthrightly.

"Oh, give him a chance," said Jeremy.

Andrew started to cry.

So obvious, the meaning of a dream like that. So blatant. She wanted everything. She wanted the boys back, but she wanted what she had now. And she wanted Owen as well.

She wanted him so much. She hadn't realised how much until now. The memory of their night together was raw and painful, but she found herself dwelling on it as she hadn't done since the last few weeks of her pregnancy. His ghost was everywhere in the house, becoming stronger even than the children's. Part of her hated him for eclipsing those other memories. It was what she had wanted, to have a reason to go on, but it hadn't turned out at all as she had planned.

The worst thing was the knowledge that, after all that had passed between them, he still preferred Jenny to her. Men were so strange. They could love one woman and make love to any number of others whilst remaining devoted to their chosen partner.

Perhaps women weren't that different though. Julia recalled that she herself had hankered after other men, including Owen, while married to Keith, without ever wanting to leave Keith or put her marriage at risk in any way. She had found it easier to resist the physical temptation to infidelity than Owen had, but she had still felt it, and strongly too. The truth was that she had wanted Owen when she knew that he was unavailable. She wouldn't have made a move to cause a split with Jenny, but now that it had happened, it seemed he was no more attainable than he had been before.

For pity's sake, he was years younger than her. He couldn't possibly be expected to prefer her to someone young and pretty, without any of the psychological encumbrances that Julia carried. His separation from Jenny was what Julia had dreamed of, but now that it had come to pass, it was just another of her nightmares.

No doubt he blamed Julia as much as he blamed himself, and rightly so. She had known exactly what she was doing. Even if it was true that Jenny hadn't found out about her and Owen, it was possible that, subconsciously, Jenny had sensed that he was hiding something from her. That, very likely, was what had driven her into the arms of another man.

Still, she owed him something, even if he didn't want to take it. How would she give it to him? All she had to offer him was money; he wanted nothing else from her, and he wouldn't take material things, because he saw it as payment for selling himself.

He would never come to her again.

CHAPTER TWENTY-EIGHT

The weeks went by.

Quite unexpectedly, Mike called. He carried an extravagant bouquet, chocolates, and a present for Imogen, a toy she wouldn't be able to appreciate for at least three years. It's the thought that counts, Julia said to herself as she opened the neatly wrapped parcel. He had been away for the Christmas and New Year holidays, he said, and had only just heard that the baby had arrived. Julia didn't ask from whom he had heard it.

It wasn't that she didn't want to see Mike, but his cheeriness somehow set her teeth on edge. He made all the right noises when viewing the baby in her cot, and stayed far longer than mere politeness demanded. There was something on his mind, she sensed that, and it had to come out.

Later, much later, when it was all over, she realised that he must have been planning this visit for some time. Probably he had known about the birth for weeks, and had been building up the courage she hadn't thought he needed, in order to confront her with his affection.

"I won't beat about the bush, Julia," he said, after having done exactly that for an hour or more. "I can see you haven't got a man around the place, though obviously I don't know your exact circumstances. You shouldn't be on your own, at a time like this. I realise you don't know me all that well, not intimately, that is, but I wanted to offer my services."

She couldn't immediately understand what he meant.

"If you want anything done around the place, or if you just want someone around, I'm your man," he continued, and paused expectantly.

"That's very kind of you," she said eventually. "I've had lots of generous offers of help and support. I don't think I'll need to trouble you, but thank you for the thought, all the same."

He looked disconcerted.

"I don't think I'm making myself clear," he said after a moment. "I mean that I want us to have some kind of relationship."

Some kind of relationship. What an odd way to put it, she thought. It was almost like drawing up a contract.

"What kind of relationship do you mean?" she asked, playing for time.

"A serious one," he replied, becoming visibly more uncomfortable by the second. "I mean, you're an attractive woman. I've always liked you. You're single, I'm single. I think you like me too. I don't mean to sound big-headed, but I think I can tell when women are attracted to me."

Big-headed or not, he made it sound as if it happened all the time. She found it hard not to smile.

"Oh." She took a long time to think out her response. For a moment, she was tempted. There would be many advantages to having Mike as Imogen's surrogate father.

"I'm sorry," she said. "There's someone else, you see."

"Ah. I suppose that would be…the baby's father?"

She nodded. "He's not with me, and not likely to be, but he's still the one, if you understand what I mean."

"I see. No need to apologise. I just thought, you know, that we could help one another out. Perhaps I was jumping the gun just a little."

"Just a little," she agreed.

"Well, you did know, didn't you, that I fa…that I was attracted to you? I haven't just sprung this on you out of the blue, have I?"

She shrugged.

"I mean," he went on, "I knew, right from the start, that you were the one."

The one? It was frightening. She had known he liked her, but to think that he cared for her with an intensity she hadn't begun to imagine was truly disturbing.

"I…er…I don't know what to say, Mike. I like you, and I know we've got on well in class—and outside of class, I suppose, but I didn't really think there was anything more than that on your side."

To do him justice, he was looking very embarrassed now, but it didn't stop him talking, or smiling. Nothing could stop Mike from smiling.

"The first time I met you, I thought, 'This one's for me,' if you know what I mean. I didn't know how you were fixed, but you never mentioned anyone, so I thought you were probably divorced, like me. I noticed you wore a wedding ring, but that doesn't really mean anything these days."

She might as well be open with him now.

"I'm not divorced. I'm a widow, you see."

"Oh!" Now he was genuinely shocked. "Oh Lord, I'm sorry. That's just…"

"I'm sorry I didn't tell you, but I just can't talk about it. Please try and understand."

They had come to some kind of compromise. Julia knew she had never been fair to Mike. Knowing that she couldn't return his feelings, she had made a deliberate effort not to lead him on, and yet it seemed she had done so. Now she had at least told him half the truth. Perhaps, after all, they could be friends.

As he got to the front door, he confronted her unexpectedly.

"Is it that guy from college?"

Julia could barely find the breath to respond. For a half-second, she retained some hope that he meant Steve Desborough, or someone equally impossible.

"From college?" she echoed weakly.

"The ginger-haired guy, the one you knew before, from the computer lab. Ewan, is it?"

"Owen," she corrected, feeling an irrational annoyance at the mistake. A denial should have sprung easily to her lips, but all she actually said was, "I don't want to talk about it. Please."

"Okay." Mike smiled, though not as broadly as was his custom. He left promising to call again. Somehow Julia didn't expect that he would.

She thought about the time when she had seriously considered asking Mike to be the father of her child, when she had been genuinely attracted to him. She couldn't remember now what had finally decided her that he was unsuitable, or whether she had consciously decided it at all. Here was a man she could have had at any time, a man who would have fathered her child and saved her from having to bother anyone else. Owen's relationship with Jenny could have survived intact, and Julia could still have had her baby. It was a cruel thought.

How had Mike known? He must be very sensitive to her moods, as he had barely set eyes on Owen. Was it that obvious, seeing the two of them together, that she was in love with Owen? Or had it merely been a lucky guess on Mike's part, Owen being the only man he knew her to be acquainted with? Her failure to deny everything had been a dead give-away. Their secret could remain intact only as long as Mike didn't mention it to anyone. It was unlikely that he knew anyone who would have been interested, but that didn't ease the feeling of having betrayed Owen.

She wondered how Owen would look in the eyes of another man, someone like Mike. It was a pointless speculation, another self-indulgent moment. There was nothing Owen had that Mike lacked. Mike was available and willing, moreover. But Mike wasn't what she wanted, and never would be. Only now could Julia see how she had manipulated both men in different ways, making excuses for herself, hurting others in order to get what she wanted.

She went back into the living room to look at Imogen, who was scraping the vinyl cot bumper with her soft fingernails in a frenzy of physical exploration. This should have been enough. It was another child Julia had wanted, not another husband. She no longer wished to die. She had everything she needed.

I am so *lucky*, she thought. How dare I ask for more? I am so *lucky*. I lost everything, and I've been given it back. I have a reason to live. It should be enough. It will have to be.

Minutes later, as she was re-filling the sterilising unit, the doorbell rang. Quickly wiping her wet hands on a towel, she crossed from the kitchen to the hall to answer the door, half-expecting it to be Mike returning. She looked quickly around the living room to see if he had left anything. Surely he wasn't going to have another try. It must be someone else.

And now, at this moment, surprising her as always, who else should it have been but the father of her child?

"Sorry to disturb you," said Owen, his voice quieter even than usual. He could barely look her in the eye. "If you're in the middle of something, I can come back."

Speechless, Julia stood aside for him to enter. As if on cue, the baby began to scream.

"Make yourself at home," she said, rushing, not thinking about the words. "I'll be with you in a moment."

He wandered into the room behind her. Picking Imogen up, Julia patted her back.

"I'm glad you came back," she said, concentrating on winding the child so that she wouldn't have to look him in the face. "I felt we hadn't parted on good terms. And I really am sorry about Jenny."

"That's okay. It doesn't matter."

She wasn't sure exactly what he meant by that, but she let it pass.

"Are you working?"

"Not yet."

"Still in the bedsit?"

"Yeah. I don't suppose I could hold the baby again, could I?"

Of course, it was Imogen that had lured him back, not any desire to see Julia. She was duly handed over to her father, who held her only slightly less awkwardly than the first time, peering into her face as though looking for something.

After the baby had stopped crying and was in the bouncy chair that just about fitted her now, they sat down.

"I wanted to check," said Owen. "I thought maybe I was imagining it the first time, that she looked like me."

"She does look like you," Julia confirmed. "Baby girls often look more like their fathers than their mothers. So they tell me, anyway. Of course, I've never had a girl before."

"Is it like you thought? Is it bringing you what you want?" he asked earnestly.

Julia thought hard. "It's a reason to live," she said. But it doesn't bring me everything I want, she could have added.

"Good." Another of those awkward pauses followed. He offered no further explanation for his presence, and she was afraid to hear one. She tried a different tack.

"Can I ask you something, Owen?"

He nodded, noncommittally.

"Did it mean anything to you? Not the first time, I mean, but that other time, after your mother died. Did that mean anything?"

"What are you on about? Of course it did!"

"But you still loved Jenny."

"Yes." He looked confused and exasperated.

"Do you hate me now?"

He fidgeted angrily. "I don't think I've done anything to deserve to have you say that to me. I don't blame you, if that's what you mean. It was me that came to you, not the other way around."

It had been building up inside her to say a certain thing, and now she knew that she would say it, even though she had resolved not to.

"Would you consider coming to live with me?"

He was genuinely taken by surprise. A flush spread over his pale features.

"How do you mean?"

"I mean, would you come and live here with me and Imogen, at least as a temporary arrangement? It could be any way you like. You could be here as her father, or just as a house-guest, it's up to you. Only I really need help."

"To do what?"

"I hadn't forgotten how tiring being a mother is, but it still caught me unawares. I don't get a minute to myself. Oh, people want to help—my mother, for example, and the woman next door. But I don't want them here all the time. I want someone to share parenthood with. If you could do that, it would be great, but if you can't, then maybe you could just help me out now and again with a few household jobs and maybe babysit occasionally. I'm not asking you for anything else. But you could live here for as long as you like, and I thought, while you're out of work, it might be some use to you, save you some money, you know…"

She had run out of words, and none of the words she had said were the ones she had meant to use. Tears began to spill out instead. Owen ignored them, seeming not to notice.

"You could have Jeremy's room," she added, catching her breath. "You'd want to re-decorate it, of course."

"Let me get this straight. You don't want me to live with you in the normal sense, I mean in the way I was living with Jenny. You just want me to be here for a while."

"That's about it. Anything else is…well, it would be unreasonable of me to expect anything else."

There was another long silence.

"If I was to come here, and then Jenny was to change her mind, I'd have to go back to her, you know."

"That would be up to you. You can stay as long as you like, and leave whenever you like."

"All right."

She hadn't thought it would be so easy to persuade him. Something told her he knew exactly what she intended. Perhaps it was really what he had wanted all along. She still wasn't sure whether it was the right thing to do. There was going to be so much explaining to do, to her parents, Edie, other people. There might be a long time to wait before he got over Jenny. But he was worth the trouble. Probably.